FIREBRAND RANGE

Johnny Travers wasn't running anymore. He'd found a spot that suited him in Arizona Territory and he intended to stay awhile—in spite of his portrait being framed on a few local trees and captioned "$2,500 Reward"—and in spite of the bounty hunters and other observant gents willing to overlook a bad conscience for that kind of money.

He wasn't going to turn tail because of the big Star Cross ranch either, the one with the 3,000 cattle and their eye on Travers' water. Nor would he turn tail for his own dubious hired gunhands or two of the prettiest reasons for leaving someplace fast.

No, Johnny Travers might do some fancy side-stepping, but he wasn't running. And when a man like Travers decides to set a spell, it's like inviting a tornado to stay for supper.

D1108721

Charter Westerns by Nelson Nye

THE NO-GUN FIGHTER
LONG RUN
THE SEVEN SIX-GUNNERS
TROUBLE AT QUINN'S CROSSING (*coming in March*)

RIDER ON
THE ROAN

NELSON NYE

CHARTER BOOKS, NEW YORK

RIDER ON THE ROAN

A Charter Book / published by arrangement with
the author

PRINTING HISTORY
Ace edition published 1967
Second printing / October 1979
Charter edition / February 1987

ISBN: 0-441-72302-0

Charter Books are published by The Berkley Publishing Group,
200 Madison Avenue, New York, New York 10016.
PRINTED IN THE UNITED STATES OF AMERICA

I

KATE BALLARD, just returned from an afternoon in the saddle, was in the barn at Star Cross rubbing down her horse and, because she was a lonely girl much given to introspection, contrasting the freedoms of the open range with her disciplined past in a dreary succession of far-off and high-priced boarding schools when the contentious voice of her uncle's range boss cut across her thoughts from the day pen outside.

He was grousing again about the long drought which, as a conversational gambit, had in Kate's opinion overstayed its welcome. Another neighbor, it seemed, had gone to the wall. But glutted markets and the current water shortage were hardly concerns which endeared themselves to an eighteen year old orphan so recently removed from the sheltering rules of the Misses Crotty's Academy for Refined Young Ladies. A month's conversations taken up with these matters had exhausted her interest.

She could not remember her parents, could scarcely visualize a time when Uncle Benny had not stood for

5

a kind of Daddy Longlegs, a ghost of Authority somewhere in Arizona Territory who presumably paid her bills, dispatched a doll each year at Christmas, a silver dollar for her birthdays, occasional stiffly cheerless letters in a crabbed hard-to-read hand filled with ranch work and don'ts and unfailingly, every Easter, was the source of a hugely elaborate chocolate egg.

"I can't see that you've got much choice," McCartrey grumbled. "That range could save our bacon, Benny."

Ballard, plainly worried, said, "This drought won't last forever."

"Keep thinkin' like that an' we'll be out of a job."

"But it isn't my fault. I've done all—"

McCartrey snorted. "You think them Scotchmen'll care about that? All they're lookin' for in Glasgow is profits. They've sunk a pot in this place. You better git the lead out!"

"I'll drive in and talk to Colter."

"You'll git no loan from him. Ranch property ain't collateral these days—the banks is stuffed with paper. We got just one out an' you know it. Crescent."

Her uncle was silent so long out there that Kate, uncomfortably conscious of being a party to matters not intended for her ears, was about to try and slip out the back door when Ballard gruffly said, "Be a hell of a thing to rough up that old man—"

"Them Luceys is trash! Shiftless, improvident, daydreamin' trash. He had that place before we come in here—him an' his precious goddam books!"

"He's peculiar. But, after all, he pioneered . . ."

McCartrey said with an ugly contempt, "That spread'll run fifteen hundred head of mother cows an' what's he doin' with it? Piddlin' round with less'n a hundred, using our bulls an sellin' the increase t' cover his expenses. Hell, some of that grass ain't never been stepped on! This mornin' I was over there tryin' t' kick up some basis for a dicker—know what he tol' me?

6

Says, 'I like it, McCartrey, just the way it is!' If it wasn't for him an' that goddam rifle—"

"That's not the point."

"Point is he's fenced off the water!" McCartrey snarled. "That spring-fed lake could save Star Cross an' that goddam grass could make us a profit!" He said with thin patience, "You wouldn't have t' rough him up any, either."

"He won't be jumped without a fight," Ballard said.

"You think he kin fight three thousan' head of cattle?" McCartrey hooted. "Alls we'd have t' do is push 'em over there. If we ship now Star Cross is gonna fold, git sold or find itself a new manager!"

A kind of silence closed down through which Kate held her breath. Her uncle said gruffly, "Just what do you propose?"

"Hell, it's all open range. Only thing he's got patent to is that water he's fenced. We could take a couple boys off the payroll. When they've filed homesteads all nice an legal spang in the middle of that ol' fool's best graze Star Cross will lease an' we'll move in the cows." The range boss said impatiently, "Hell, you can't lose!"

"What about water?" Ballard asked uneasily.

McCartrey laughed. "They'll water at his lake. He's got no help an' no money to hire any. Oh, he'll shoot a few, sure, but he'll not throw 'em back. You've heard 'em bawlin'. They'll—"

"He *owns* that water. He'll take us to court."

"So what if he does? You can't have everything. But we'll have the grass an' the water to hold it! Let him scream. Possession round here is nine points of the law, an' we'll have possession. Three thousan' head of thirst crazed critters ain't t' be stopped by wavin' no writ at 'em!"

"I don't like it," Ballard growled.

"Them cows'll like it. An' while the shysters argue they'll be puttin' on weight. If you're goin' t' stay big you

7

gotta take a few chances. Christ! what can he prove?"

"Well . . ." Ballard said as they started to move off. "Better not use any Star Cross punchers."

"Plenty of bums a guy can hire for peanuts—"

"I dont want to know how you do it. Just fatten them steers and let me know when they're ready."

Kate Ballard that night didn't do much sleeping. She spent the most of it twisting, hard tugged two ways between what she felt was owed to her uncle and what conscience told her was the right thing to do.

There was no use going to Benny about it. Drought and the range boss had him over a barrel.

She had not yet come to any clear-cut decision when McCartney and the crew in advance of full light rode out to take care of the day's pressing chores.

When the sun came above the distant Cherrycow ramparts to rouse the valley's birds and flood her room with its invigorating warmth Kate was still besieged and uncomfortably conscious of the considerable disparity between the way things seemed and how any right-minded person must know they had ought to be.

She could not excuse her uncle's complaisance, and was still in a turmoil over what she had heard. She had her full share of youth's illusions, little experience to call on and loyalty, she was finding, could be a two-edged sword. But there were precepts to guide one. The course between obligation and what one saw as one's plain bounden duty—no matter how repugnant—was inevitably clear. Two wrongs did not ever make a right.

She finally got up and put on her clothes. Avoiding the mirror, she ran a comb through her hair, hungry because, in no mood to face her uncle last night, she had come to her room without stopping for supper.

Never the earliest of risers she was quite accustomed to fixing her own breakfast but was somewhat surprised to find the office door open and the big house, except for herself, completely empty.

After eating and washing the things she had used she picked up the cowboy hat Benny had bought her, slipped out the back door and, not without some feelings of guilt, stole across to the barn and hurriedly readied her horse.

Despite all the woolling around she had given it she still wasn't sure how best to approach this, but something had to be done. That much was plain. From what she had heard, riding over to warn Old Man Pete Lucey looked a complete waste of time. Because what could she tell him without implicating her uncle? He apparently wasn't in any position to help himself anyway.

So someone else must intervene.

Obviously she could not go to the sheriff.

But she had to go *somewhere*. In her state of mind she couldn't stand still.

Wildflower wasn't much to look at, just a weather-beaten huddle of sunbleached frames and box square adobes their owners hadn't even bothered to plaster. Thirty-four homes, two stores, five saloons, a gun shop, hat shop, a six-room hotel. Yet it served an area bigger than some states and was connected by stage to Tombstone, Tucson, Willcox and Douglas. It had just two things to recommend it to Travers. It wasn't a county seat and it was a long way from Ehrenberg as the appearance of his travel gaunted gelding amply attested.

His dust-coated clothes were of the condition and variety all too often seen on penniless range bums, of which Wildflower regrettably had certainly seen its quota. From disreputable floppy-brimmed hat to the runover heels of brush scarred boots he would hardly have rated a second glance, an effect Mr. Travers had been at some pains to cultivate. He didn't *want* to be noticed, but he'd forgotten one thing. It had slipped his mind that a man generally carries, along with other pertinent parts of his anatomy, the blandishments and habits which have made him what he is.

All his life Johnny Travers had been a gambler. Not the saddle blanket kind. Not the hairline moustached sort of smoky room tinhorn glimpsed in black string tie and ruffled shirt beneath some barroom's hanging lamp—but just as proud and twice as deadly if you put any stock in the way some told it.

He was a man who liked a long-odds game.

This proclivity had been largely responsible for most of the pleasures he had found along the way. That it was also the source of his present predicament had somehow escaped his eagle eyed notice.

While entirely consistent with the nature of his exploits he could scarcely deny the jolt of discovering, the morning after that business at Ehrenberg, his face staring back at him from one of those advertisements law enforcement officers tack to posts and public hoardings.

What he read in black print was *WANTED FOR MURDER!*

Travers hadn't stopped to pack any bag.

It made no difference that the tempting reward, along with the broadsheets, had been put up by kin of the deceased—that he'd left the victim vociferously howling. Close kin and heirs sometimes take it rather badly when some outsider happens to get there first and decamps with their expectancy.

They couldn't have cared less who had killed the bastard. It was the loot, not the death, that had built this fire under him. The guy had probably shot himself—not that it made a particle of difference.

Bounty hunters seldom showed much interest in particulars.

Travers looked around. A hotel wasn't much use to him now but he did like what he saw of this place.

10

As hub and purchasing center of a back country area devoted to cows and mining this town was just about lively enough to have concerns more crucial than keeping tabs on drifters.

With reasonable care a man could lose himself here.

Comforted some, he considered the saloons, turning away from what appeared to be the largest, reining his ewe-necked blue roan toward a dingier place beside Ogleby's Mercantile considerably closer to the street's far end, reminded by past experience of the conversational tidbits a man might pick up while resting his boot on the rail of a bar.

He was nearly there when a brown haired girl in divided skirt and cow-country hat, bound across the dust of the road, stepped away from the tie rack fronting the Mercantile. At which precise moment a man, violently driven through the saloon's burst-open batwings, came reeling, back pedaling, across the boardwalk to flop hard on his butt not two feet from the girl, who stopped frozen with dismay.

Cursing, the man began to pick himself up.

The batwings cracked again to reveal the other half of this argument, a hulking brute in miner's shirt who, grinning nastily, said, "Just remember what I told you, Fraskens. Don't come sloshin' in here again."

The man, half up, snarling, went for his gun.

Travers, conscious only of the danger to the girl, dug in his spurs with a Comanche yell.

It locked the man in his tracks, head twisting. The guy in the batwings ducked from sight and along the walk there were duckers, too, as Travers, bending, swept up the girl and rode her out of the line of fire.

II

ACROSS THE STREET he set her down and they stared at each other, breathing hard. She had lost her hat. Wind ruffled her hair.

Travers, now that he had time to notice, found her shapely, firm with youth, a little tall for a girl. She was not what he would have called "a looker." There were dozens of frails with light brown hair. Green eyed ones, too, with better noses.

He did become rather interested in her mouth. Mouths could tell you a lot about a person and hers seemed somehow strangely wistful, a bit worried, unsure. Without being full her lips hinted at things she'd never put into words.

The girl, too, was arrested by what she saw. A man of medium height in dusty range clothes and brush clawed boots—dark sun-streaked hair when he hauled off his hat to say, "Sorry if I startled you. Flying lead don't give a whoop who it smacks into." He shucked a grin. "I'm Johnny Travers."

"Kate Ballard," she said, still considering him.

His eyes were an alert gray that looked hard as slate. He rested his weight on the swell of the saddle, openly returning her appraising stare in the frank way of men not too often around a woman. He had strong white teeth and there was in the look of them a bold sort of recklessness that almost unnerved her.

He swung down. "I'll fetch your hat."

Her stare reached after him, wondering, fearful. She found in his horse the same hard signs of travel. A stranger then, a man not caught up in things which concerned this drought or her uncle. A man without ties.

He came back with her hat, watched her put it on primly. And climbed into the saddle.

She peered at him anxiously. Smile too bright—either nerves or embarrassment. Probably inordinately shy; her efforts to cover this made her seem awkward.

She suddenly blurted, "Would you do something for me?"

"Pardon?"

"You look like a man who wouldn't mind a little risk." She stared at him aghast, took a further hurried plunge before natural reticence and fears of her uncle's wrath could choke off the rush of words. "There's something has to be done . . . it calls for a man or I would do it myself. It must be done quickly—I mean he's got to be warned and backed up to defy them. It's nothing *illegal!*"

She thought the way he stared he must imagine that she had a spool loose. "It's that poor old man," she cried, "Pete Lucey. They're going to take his lake away from him!"

Travers' eyes thinned down as they searched her face. She couldn't guess at his thoughts but, at least, she had his interest. "Maybe," he said, "you'd better start at the beginning," and got out of his saddle. "Let's get off this street." He took her arm. "Where's a good place to eat?"

She knew very little more than he did about what was good or bad in this town. In the end, leading his dilapidated horse which they left out front, they settled on the hotel dining room. Except for a couple of loud talking drummers catching up on laughs they had the place to themselves.

Travers picked out a table off against the far wall, telling the waitress when she came with her shoo-fly to throw on a pair of steaks and not to smother them in onions.

"Now, what about this feller?" he said, and "Keep your voice down."

That there was risk involved appeared pretty obvious from the lip-nibbling way she continued to eye him while marshaling her story. He guessed she might be having two or three belated doubts about confiding in him at all.

"It's your move," he smiled, not much caring one way or the other except as this might find him a reasonable excuse for lingering in this neighborhood.

"It's this drought," she said. "I think it's bringing out a side of folks I hadn't guessed existed."

Travers thought about that and nodded. "When you nick a man's pocketbook you dig him in the quick."

Prodded by shrewd questions he finally got her talking and the picture that emerged—as much from what she left out as from stark facts enumerated—was of a potty old settler perched on patented water which the wolves had got their eyes on. That homesteading bit was an old dodge easily recognized; more than just a few cow raisers had hoisted themselves into baron's boots through enlarging their holdings in some such fashion.

"And where do I fit in?" Travers asked bluntly.

"I—I thought perhaps you could be one of the homesteaders."

"That wouldn't help your friend much."

She watched him, worrying, not knowing what to say hardly. He saw her mouth tighten when he asked, "Who *are* these fellers?—the ones that want that water?"

When it looked as though she wouldn't answer he said, "If I'm going to be any help at all I've got to know all I can find out about it. Why don't this Lucey hire himself some help?"

"He doesn't know—"

"Then why didn't you go straight to him with your story?"

"It wouldn't do any good," she said, gnawing her lip. "He can't fight off three thousand head of cattle and he can't hire help. He hasn't got any money."

"Oh, fine!" Travers said, looking down his nose at her. "So what do I get out of risking my neck?"

She stared at the napkin her hands had been twisting. "I hadn't thought of that." Her eyes examined him again. "It seems I'm not very practical."

Travers have her a sharp look and grunted. "For a girl," he said, "brought up in cow country—"

"But I'm not—I wasn't!" Flushing painfully she cried, "I've only been here a month . . ." and stopped, mouth open, surprised and dismayed. She hadn't intended saying so much. Now that it was out she said in obvious confusion, "Father—my mother . . . I'm an orphan, you see. All my life I've been away at schools."

She saw Travers' brows climb. "They've got a boarding school *here*?"

She giggled from nervousness, flushing, shook her head. "Of course not! That was back East . . . in the States," she said primly. "I'm staying with my uncle."

"At Star Cross," he nodded, pleased to note he'd hit the target.

It was like he'd pulled a rabbit from her hat. She said, in shock: "You're acquainted with Uncle Benny?"

Travers shook his head. The waitress came with their steaks, the platters garnished with potatoes and puckered peas poured out of cans. Travers said when she left, "Wouldn't know him from Adam," and picked up his eating tools. "I came in from that direction, saw signs of overgrazing, a heap of Star Cross cattle. If somebody's after a lake in this country it's dollars to doughnuts it had to be him."

She continued to stare. "I suppose I've been pretty silly." He saw the worry in her eyes. She flushed again and licked dry lips. "I expect you know I wouldn't want this to get back to him. . . ."

15

Travers shrugged. "Be surprised if you did." He looked up to say dryly, "Better figure, however, it's got around by now that Benny's niece is in here eating with some drifter."

She said, "Considering the way he rushed in to save me when that fellow in the street made a grab for his pistol the very least I could do was offer him a meal." She smiled at him demurely.

Travers stared. He was not a man to be easily surprised but the way she had pulled that out of the blue seemed to indicate a need for some careful rethinking. He studied her uncomfortably. "What kind of a game are you playing with me, Missy?"

This produced another blush and he returned her stare with considerable distrust. "If you're setting me up to be some kind of fall guy . . ."

Her eyes showed distaste and he saw scorn in the tightening roll of her lips. "If that remark suggests what I think it does it's apparent we've nothing more to say to each other."

"You couldn't be more wrong," Travers growled and, as she reached for her gloves, caught her hand at the wrist. "Sit down and bite into that steak," he said gruffly. "If I've spoke out of turn you have my apology."

She appeared of two minds but finally relaxed enough to pick up her fork. After a moment she said, "I haven't heard any shots. What do you suppose happened out there?"

"Nothing. Big bruiser in the doorway ducked back out of sight—other one thought better of his notion, I'd imagine."

He'd begun to think the whole deal was rigged, but now he wasn't so sure. She didn't look that kind of girl, not really; she certainly was young enough to have just finished school. And those blushes . . .

She sighed. "I guess I'm not cut out for this. Playing the part of Good Samaritan takes a lot more fortitude

16

than I'd imagined. When I overheard McCartrey hatching that plan to get rid of Pete Lucey all I could think of was that defenseless old man."

"The principle of the thing."

"I suppose so."

"Who's McCartrey?"

"My uncle's foreman. He doesn't own Star Cross, you know; he's just the manager. This drought, I guess, has hit them pretty hard. But to take that old man's lake away and steal his grass . . ."

Travers nodded. "You were outraged when Benny agreed to go along with it."

"It was pretty upsetting to think your own uncle—"

"Sure," Travers said. "I can understand that. But . . ."

"You can't understand, with nothing to offer, why I'd suppose you'd be interested in helping—"

"That's about the size of it," Travers said, watching her.

"I seem to be rather impulsive. I came into town intending to warn him but he's in no position to help himself. He's sort of a hermit. He's got a few cows and lives by selling his increase each year. I was thinking about this when that fellow—but I suppose you'll ride on . . . ?"

It wasn't a question exactly but the suggestion was there in the way her green eyes peered into his own. It was a lot like showing a red rag to a bull. There were more ways than one to fence a man in and he narrowed his look with a touch of resentment. His distrust grew apace but the challenge still showed in the fold of her lips.

He growled at her irritably and did some hard thinking while he cut up the rest of his steak and ate it. Then he pushed back his chair and got out the makings. It was hard to believe a nice girl like her would deliberately toll a man into a trap . . . and he could use some cover if he aimed to stay on here.

17

She gave him a frustrated look and got up.

Travers said gruffly, "Leave some change on the table. I'll mosey on out there."

III

AFTER SHE'D GONE Travers finished his smoke, stubbed the butt in his plate and, tipping the disreputable hat across his eyes, went outside and got on his horse, typical picture of the penniless drifter.

He was far from being greatly pleased with himself for he still felt the challenge of that green stare. You couldn't hardly say he was actually committed; all he'd promised was to go have a look, yet it seemed to him somehow he was being maneuvered—and that didn't make any kind of sense, either.

On his ewe-necked roan he sat at the tie rail some additional moments, giving the town a chance to look him over while he scowlingly contemplated the double line of drab buildings without discovering any sign of the surly gun-grabber whose recent activity had propelled Travers into this. While he looked he reviewed what the girl had told him and what going along with it might ultimately cost.

Hell, she wasn't even his kind of woman! Just a gawky, mixed-up kid, still damp behind the ears and about as nervous a proposition as he had ever run into. Every instinct warned him away from this, yet what she had said made a kind of grim sense. No kid her age could be that good a fooler. She'd probably told him the truth.

Or what she thought was the truth.

He wheeled his roan from the pole, sent it shuffling

between flanking walks, conning again the passersby and the danger he felt to be threading this wind blowing off the distant Cherrycow rim. It was not the sort of setup any guy in his boots with a lick of sense would consider for a minute, but therein lay the real pull of it. Or so, grinning sourly, he managed to believe.

No pictures of him had been posted here, and who would suspect any fool bucking Star Cross—obviously the biggest spread in these parts—to be on the run from a charge of murder? If he stayed, though, he thought, it might be just as well to pick up a new name. Even if there wasn't any sheriff's office here.

Swinging down in front of the Mercantile, which had a Post Office sign under the proprietor's name, he tossed his reins across the hitch rail and went inside. The store was fairly crowded, the customers keeping three clerks hopping. After a cursory look to make sure that jasper, Fraskens, wasn't among them he stepped over to the mail window, asking the girl behind the grill if she could tell him where he might find Pete Lucey.

Looking a little surprised, she said he could likely be found at his ranch and indifferently gave him directions for reaching it.

Thanking her, Travers quit the store for the porch and, on the top step, paused with narrowing glance. Beside Travers' roan a pair of men were posted in watchful absorption while a third—the burly brute that fellow Fraskens had been about to engage with flying lead—stood pawing through Travers' untied blanket roll.

Travers' thoughts spun through split seconds. He said, spider soft: "Enjoying yourselves?"

The watching pair went rigidly stiff. The searcher, coolly ignoring his words, went right along with it, even, scowl deepening, to giving slicker and blankets a vigorous shake before tossing them contemptuously across Travers' saddle.

"Put 'em back the way you found 'em."

The rock hard edge in Travers' voice now fetched the searcher round to where the sun threw a flash from metal pinned to his vest. The man's eyes flicked Travers' expressionless face in a twisting upward insolent look. "Where's the gun?" he said, lips skinned back from big teeth.

"Put 'em back," Travers said from the top of the steps.

For a couple of heartbeats violence hung by a thread, then the burly man with his lips clamped together re-rolled Travers' belongings and tied them snugly behind the saddle. Then he faced about, the top half of his body bent a little from the hips, arms hanging straight down. On the porch back of Travers someone scuttled inside.

"Now," said the marshal, "I'll take a look at that gun."

"You'll have to *take* it," Travers smiled.

The silence stretched, became exceedingly uncomfortable while curious pedestrians on the flanking walks stood stiff as stones in the unnatural hush and the man's two companions huddled worriedly beside him.

But the marshal's curiosity did not appear to be that acute. He pulled out of his crouch with a covering sneer. "Tough guy, eh? Stick around here till dark and we'll see how tough you are," he said shortly and, beckoning his men, strode off up the street.

Travers, ignoring the curious stares, came down the steps and climbed into the saddle. Silently cursing the stiff-necked pride which had settled him so strongly into these people's minds he wheeled the roan from the tie rack and sent him shambling toward the other end of town.

But he was not immersed in his own sour reflections so completely as to forget the needs of his horse. At a feed corral at the community's western edge he stopped long enough to buy the roan a forkful of hay, a half bucket of oats and a few moments' stand beside a trough filled with water.

He camped out that night, not because Lucey was too far to get to but because for a number of reasons he preferred to arrive in broad light of day. He recalled what had been said about the old man's rifle and he wanted, too, to find out if he'd been followed by that bullypuss marshal or the pair that had been with him.

He built up no fire to advertise his whereabouts and when he spread his blankets it was in the thorny cover of a thicket of mesquites. He could picture that marshal pawing through his stacks of dodgers and could only hope this end of the cactus was far enough removed from the sphere of vengeful relatives to have been ignored or completely bypassed by any spreaders of his likeness.

The night passed without incident.

Coming out of his hideyhole he managed a leisurely coffeeless breakfast from dried-out stuff packed around in his pockets. If nothing for taste it did keep his backbone from rubbing his navel. And while he chewed he kept his eyes busy hunting for dusts which might have sprung from some vengeance nearer.

The only dust spotted was a good ways off in the direction of Star Cross, probably stirred by Ballard punchers moving out to get started on the new day's chores.

It occurred to Travers that the Star Cross range boss, with his job to look out for, would not be one to waste any time putting things in motion for the grab of that lake Lucey watched with his rifle.

He collected his horse, took off the hobbles and climbed aboard.

Instead of proceeding about his business he struck off at a tangent on a three-mile swing which in due course

21

intercepted the tracks he'd made coming from town. After several passes back and forth across these tracks it seemed pretty likely he had not been followed. But he had not survived a career in long odds by complacently accepting appearances for facts. Hawk-eyed, he continued his circle through a rash of sprawled hogbacks to come back on the stage road some miles south of where he had left it. Only then, reassured, did he strike out for Crescent.

The road kept winding, gradually climbing as it left the rough country by a series of spurs from which lesser roads angled off through live oak and sycamores toward various small spreads hidden from sight. Just before he got into the pines, in the footslopes now of the towering Cherrycows, the southbound stage rocked past on its thoroughbraces with a whoop and a holler flinging dust hat high.

He got off the road for it, still playing cautious, unwilling to contribute any cards he didn't have to. Truly interested parties would be discovering his whereabouts much too soon regardless; it was in the very nature of this chore he'd set his hand to.

Though he'd been woolling it around he had thus far dug up no way to put an efficacious spoke in the wheel of Star Cross plans. No one man, as the girl had reported McCartrey telling Ballard, was going to fight off three thousand head of thirst crazed cattle. Nor any two men, either!

The day was fresh and still with the smell of pine pitch wafting round him like a perfume. Every detail of this uncluttered country appeared much as Indians had earlier found it, untarnished, vivid and wholly pleasant. These sights fed his senses in a way entirely strange to him, nourishing a hunger he did not comprehend, bringing him a comfort that astonished and delighted. He had quit Ehrenberg to lose himself in the vastness of the desert, to seek surcease, to find ease and rest, a quiet and a peace his hectic years had never known; yet the echoes of his past remained, stirred afresh by his meeting with Kate Ballard and the malevolent hate in that marshal's stare. He was, he knew, trapped again in that pattern of trouble he had known all his days.

A bend in the road fetched him out of the trees where the ground fell away to disclose on his right a considerable vista of spread-out country tumbling down to the sparkling gleam of bright blue water. He saw the buildings then and correctly guessed that this was Crescent, and sat there a spell taking his long and careful look. There was a solution here if a man could only find it. Travers sensed this strongly, feeling even more the notion that at last he was coming home. This was *his* kind of country. It perked up his spirits as nothing else could have.

He lingered, loath to leave the view.

Everything he saw about the place enchanted him. Sure, the buildings were hardly more than shacks, thrown up jerrybuilt and badly dilapidated within easy reach of the pole corrals. A few cattle dotted the emerald flats, halfheartedly browsing in grass that came clean up to their bellies. No wonder Star Cross hankered for this place. It was the nearest thing to a cow raiser's paradise Travers had seen.

He reluctantly brought his eyes back to the present. Ahead a trail left the road in glimpsed twists to snake down to the lake through oak brush and piñons but he passed this up, not caring to leave his sign so plain. Where the road bent again in its upward climb before straightening out for the long drop toward Dos Cabezas he eased the blue roan off the nearer flank, picking a careful way through brush and rocks, content to take whatever time was needed. This was breathtaking travel when a single misstep could plunge man and horse to a final rest where nothing but vultures would be like to discover them.

It was slow, sweaty work with those depths reaching for them and he presently swung down to cautiously lead the nervous horse past some of the twists that looked more impassable, always angling as best he could to get back to the trail now that he'd bypassed the rim. He was halfway down before this could be managed and the blue roan heaved a gust of relief when its trembling legs at last found firm ground.

Travers, too, found need of some rest and, dropping his hip to a boulder, perched at the side of the trail to take watchful stock of the headquarters area. Nothing moved near the buildings. Except for that thin twist of smoke coming out of a whoppyjawed stovepipe he'd have been inclined to think there was nobody home.

And maybe there wasn't. Pens looked empty. No horses in sight. Old boy was probably out riding his range, hunting strays. One-man spread could keep a fellow really humping.

A twinge of envy got into Travers' look as he considered this peaceful scene. Lucey, apparently, had found his niche. This might represent no vast ambition in the scale of relative values but at least you could sense a satisfied mind.

Back in the saddle Travers eased the roan houseward, still examining the view, giving thoughtful attention to possible avenues of escape. So engrossed was he with this pursuit of thought that he was considerably chagrined when, having dismounted for a soft approach, he was asked at the door while reaching for the latch, "What do you figure to be doin' there, mister?"

To be caught flat-footed was disgrace enough. To be taken by a female disconcerted him worse—nor did the fear he detected make him feel any better. He could only assume she had him under a gun, and a gun in the hands of a jittery adolescent was one of the poorest insurance risks a man could encounter.

Being not at all anxious to find himself hellbent for a coffin, Travers froze in his tracks, for several seconds scarcely breathing. "Well," he said lamely, "I thought the place was empty."

"Empty or not," she growled at him hotly, "it's considered good manners approaching a house to sing out, clear and loud. And to stay in the saddle till you're asked to get down!"

He couldn't argue with that.

"You want to try for that gun now's as good a time as any."

"You've got me all wrong," Travers sweatily protested. "I'm here to do you folks a favor—"

"Oh. A Greek bearing gifts. That sounds real likely!"

"I came to see your father—this *is* the Lucey place, isn't it?"

"You're doing the talking."

Travers swallowed uncomfortably. "If you'd let me turn around—"

"I like you fine just the way you are. And if you've anything to say you'd better say it quick before all the patience runs out of my finger."

Boots crunched gravel coming around the far side of the shack. A hearty voice whimsically boomed, "Well, now, Lupita! I see you've managed to get yourself a man."

"Not sure, Paw. This varmint smells more like skunk to me. He was about to walk into the house when I stopped him. Fixing to make himself right to home."

"Well, let's hear what he's got to say for himself. Turn around, son, and let's have a look at you."

The girl had hold of a gun all right. Big Colt's .44 with a cut-down barrel. She stood six strides away with it pointed square at him.

She looked about the same age as Kate Ballard.

Prettier, though. Smaller boned, too, with a pixie-like, big eyed face set off by a mop of taffy colored hair that she wore sheared short, not much longer than her father's collar-length fringe. You could see the family resemblance even behind that sandy beard, though the man in his prime must have topped six feet and looked broad enough yet to hunt bears with a switch.

Travers said rustily, "I'm looking for Pete Lucey."

The man shifted his cud. "You'll not get much nearer. What's on your mind, friend, besides that hat?"

"Star Cross is figuring to jump your lake."

The old man stared for several moments in silence but did not look to be particularly surprised. "Which end of Star Cross—Ballard or McCartrey?"

"McCartrey, it seems, sold the notion to Ballard." Travers slanched another nervous glance at the girl. "You mind telling her to put that thing up?"

The old man chuckled. "She couldn't hit a barn door."

IV

"Barn doors don't bother me."

Lucey grinned. A yawn stretched his mouth, and half shut eyes considered Travers shrewdly above a lifted hand that spread to hide his chin. He let the hand massage his jowls. "Seems you know an uncommon lot about the intentions of folks that don't confide in strangers. Can't hardly blame her for being some suspicious." He whipped out his thin question. "Just what are you expecting to get out of this, mister?"

"You always look a gift horse in the mouth?"

"You're the first of that breed to come my way. I figure to look you over pretty thorough." His eyes were sharp as probing knives. "You didn't just ride out here to do me a favor."

"That's right," Travers said. "I came out here to see how the deal stacked up. Looks like what I heard was no bum steer. As things stand now you haven't got a prayer."

"I'm touched by your solicitude." Lucey showed a cold grin. "Guess the next step's to offer me your indispensable services."

"Wrong," Travers said. "I offer to buy you out."

They inspected each other through a stretch of clear silence. "You know," Lucey said, "I'm beginning to enjoy you. Nothing so refreshing has popped into my lap since—"

"Put a price on it," Travers said.

"You've got no takers. Why don't you try this on Box 4 or Double N?"

"They got a lake to throw in?"

Lucey pushed back his hat to run a hand through tow hair. "You've really done your homework, haven't you? What did you say the name was, friend?"

It was Travers' turn to hesitate. He thought of those broadsheets thick around Ehrenberg. "Johnny Travers."

"You say that like it ought to ring bells." Lucey's lips came apart in a smile.

"You can't fight three thousand head of cattle. With nothing but Miss Fiesty here and no money for help," Travers said to him coolly.

Pete Lucey laughed. "Put that gun up, Pita. Fellers like this don't come by every day." He considered Travers through a cooler run of stillness. "All I've got is this lake," he said, "but I'm too old now to want to look at new country."

"I can understand that but you haven't much choice. Star Cross is big. Too much weight and too much influence for any broke old man to hope to stand up to.

27

In the face of this drought I'm surprised they haven't run over you already."

"Maybe they didn't have a smart jigger like you to dig up the right answers."

Travers said, "They've got one now. They're going to talk two fellers into setting up housekeeping spang in the heart of your best graze. It won't be strictly legal but, soon as these galoots have got their acreage filed, Star Cross'll lease their grass and move the whole operation. If you can't see where that'll leave you—"

"They can't get away with it!" the girl cried, furious, while her father squinted through half shut eyes.

"They can," Travers said, "and will unless . . ."

"He's right," Lucey said. "All we can do is go down fighting."

"What's the matter with the law? Why can't we demand protection?"

Her father looked at her, shaking his head. "The law," he said regretfully, "is people and 'protection' is as far as they're like to look. How many votes can they expect from a washed-up school teacher and a seventeen year old girl? There's your answer."

"Wrong," Travers said. "There's another one. Me."

Lucey looked him over once again but without any hopeful change of expression. "I'm afraid, Mr. Travers, you're a born optimist."

"Alone," the girl said, "you'd be no better off than we are—"

"I like to think that's open to argument." Travers said to her father, "If you won't sell out will you sell a half interest?"

The old man pressed his mouth together. Though his lips still held the faint shadow of his smile you could sense the uneasiness tramping around in him. "How much will you pay to have a piece of this fight?"

"How much do you want?"

Lucey pawed at his face. "You're the one that wants into this."

"All right. For half the brand, including lake, range and cattle, and the final say as to what's to be done with them, I'll give you ten thousand dollars."

The old man stared at him. The girl stared, too. With grudging admiration Pete Lucey said, "For a feller that don't look to have ten nickels in his jeans—"

"Never mind that, you'll get the money. Cash in hand."

It was all too apparent they didn't believe this. "I've got more than that on me right now," Travers growled at them irritably, and patted the money belt under his shirt.

"Then you ought to have yourself bored for the simples," Lucey said with blunt honesty. "The whole damn place, everything included, wouldn't fetch ten thousand on a booming market!"

"So I'm a goddam fool. You going to be one, too?"

Lucey, with a cheekful of forgotten tobacco, pulled aside his beard to hawk and spit. "I've been on the short end of the stick too long not to smell a red herring when it goes past my nose." He peered at Travers caustically. "I expect you've not mentioned all you've got in your head; so any final say, if I take your money, will have to be arrived at by a three-way vote. Yours, mine, and the girl's."

Travers dredged up a scowl. "You wouldn't be aiming to cramp my style?"

"From what I've seen it could use some cramping," Old Man Lucey said with a snort. "I may be shiftless but I can add two and two. There's things in your mind you don't mean for me to know. Maybe it's just as well," he declared, "but you're no common drifter, son. If you want cards it will be on the basis of just what I said. Take it or leave it."

Travers twisted his head to throw a look at the girl. Her eyes—they'd looked black first off—were tawny pools of unreadable flame, taking their color from her mood or surroundings. Changeable eyes, almost Mongoloid, he thought with a sudden sense of shock; and her cheekbones, too, seemed higher and broader than the average run, as though she might have Aztec or Yaqui blood.

She was an unknown quantity in more ways than one, and if he accepted Lucey's terms she would have to be reckoned with.

V

"WELL?" Lucey asked gruffly. "You want in or don't you?"

In the vision of riches conjured by Travers' offer the man's whole attitude appeared to have changed. From the way his jaw was wrapped around that cud—the fretful sound of his voice—one might almost imagine he had the stranger over a barrel. Perhaps he *was* inclined toward that notion. A calculative something, very like guile, peering out of the old man's frowning inspection suggested to Travers he might have been too quick with too much.

"I guess not," he said, watching Lucey's jaw drop, and reached for his stirrup. "A man would have to be pretty stupid to take on Star Cross with his hands tied like that."

He put his foot in the oxbow and climbed into leather. "I expect there are other spreads that don't have such hazards."

When the old man discovered that he was going to ride off he pawed at his beard in astonished confusion. Travers couldn't guess what the girl thought about it but saw her clutch the old hypothecator's arm.

Travers tipped his hat. "Been nice meetin' you." And turned the horse.

The roan was just beginning to dig in his hooves where the ground was rising in its climb toward the road when Lucey growled like a caught fence crawler. "Hold on!" he shouted, and Travers pulled up. But he did not go back—didn't even look around until the old man, wheezing like a bursted bellows, came stumbling up to catch at his stirrup.

"Maybe," he puffed, when he got back some of his breath, "I didn't make myself entirely clear to you, Travers."

"Well, let's see," Travers drawled as though collecting his thoughts. "Way I got it you're not against a part interest if I'm willing to be hamstrung at every turn."

Pete Lucey looked shocked. "No wonder you was acting like a bee got up your pantsleg! What I meant, son," he said solemn as a judge, "was that we couldn't just turn the spread plumb over to a stranger. That three-way business would be just till we got to know you. You can understand that."

"I could try," Travers nodded, but did not look enthusiastic. "When a man drops ten thousand into a losing proposition he expects to have hold of the grip end of the stick."

"And you'll have it," declared Lucey. "You'll be Crescent's ramrod. In matters concerning the range, help or cattle you'll be top man. We'll go to town right away and draw up the papers. . . ."

"I'm quite capable of dealing with double-crossers. Any papers we need can get along without lawyers," Travers said flatly, looking down at him coldly. "As for the rest, you haven't any range you can hold, and damn few cattle. How soon could we scare up some help if I want it?"

"Why—" Lucey said nervously, "Soon's you want to put up the price, I guess."

Travers grinned dryly. "You drive a hard bargain, friend. Are there any more strings you want to put on this deal?"

Lucey shook his head.

"Let's have it straight out then. For ten thousand dollars, plus pay for any help I may hire, exactly what am I getting?"

"A full half of Crescent, including land, stock and buildings. And the brand, of course."

"Yeah," Travers said. "And what about authority?"

The old man, looking worried, hedged. "I'd just want to kind of guide your hand. After all, I know these people."

"To all intents and purposes then I'd be the boss?"

Lucey, seeming profoundly uncomfortable, finally managed a reluctant nod.

"And your daughter'll agree?"

"Christ!" Lucey snapped. "She's my daughter, ain't she!"

"All right. Put it in writing and you've got yourself a partner."

He followed the old man back to the girl and remained on his horse while Lucey went inside to draw up the contract. It wasn't exactly what he wanted but he reckoned, if he could find the right kind of help, he could shave a few corners so long as he paid them. The main thing right now was to get moved in, to become known roundabout as a partnership rancher. Probably wouldn't fool the law if any badges got mixed up in this ruckus—they had means of finding out things, but it could put off those bounty hunting bastards if one of that tribe came nosing around. Travers devoutly hoped and had reason to believe he had fiddled up his tracks enough to be rid of such, but if one came along he would hardly be looking for his man among the owners.

He became aware of the girl's regard and felt uneasily astonished at the intensity of her interest, increasingly graveled at the frankness with which she permitted him to discover this. He had met most kinds in his rolling stone travels but had never found time for more than casual relationships and did not propose to extend his knowledge now. She was a wild one all right, he thought, peering back at her.

Lupita was Mex for something or other, which probably meant she'd had a Mexican mother; and this line of thought put him in mind of Kate Ballard again, also motherless and pretty mixed up if judged by what little he had seen of her. This country for sure was hell on women, but he'd things to think of here a lot more important than a couple of frails.

Hauling his glance back to Lucey, who had just come out waving two papers to dry the ink on them, Travers was more than somewhat aggravated to sense the girl's continued scrutiny—feller'd think she'd never seen a man before!

"All set?" he called to her father.

"I'll need your name on one of these," Lucey said, handing up the papers with a pen and an unstoppered bottle of muddy ink. Travers read both copies, shoved one in his pocket and, folding the other one over on a knee, wrote his name in a saddle cramped scraggle.

"Where you off to?" the old man growled as Travers started to pick up his reins. "Ain't you forgetting something?"

"The money? Hell's fire! You're not planning to keep that around here, are you?"

"I'm sure not putting it in no damned bank!"

Travers stared at him, shrugged and, reaching inside his shirt, brought forth a sheaf of bills that puckered the old man's face like a quince. "You're not fixing to pay me with that kind of stuff?"

"Anything the matter with it?"

"This here's a hard cash country. Folks around here is distrustful of paper. . . ."

Travers, ignoring him, went on with his counting, got some more from the belt and stuffed three leftover goldbacks into the pocket with the signed agreement. "You know how much weight that would make in hard money? A heap more than I'd want to pack around regular. If you're suspicious of paper any bank will change it."

Lucey reluctantly accepted the currency but not without a dissatisfied scowl. "What if the place catches fire or something?"

"That's your lookout. Safest place for cash money is a bank."

"Humph," Lucey sneered. "I notice you ain't keeping yours in no bank!"

"You might also notice I'm not trusting any hole in the ground with it, either," Travers said coolly. "And, just to make sure you don't pick up no wild notions, perhaps youd better take a good look at this."

Lucey never did guess quite where it had come from but found himself suddenly peering, drop jawed, down the cavernous bore of a fully cocked pistol.

"F' Chrissake, son," he gasped, white faced and shaken, "you tryin' to fetch me a stroke or somethin'?"

"I just want you to know I'm a mighty light sleeper." Travers dropped the gun into a baggy coat pocket and picked up his reins. "Aside from Wildflower what's the closest place to do a tolerable amount of shopping and how do I get there?"

VI

Big difference between Willcox and most of the other wide places around the Sulphur Springs valley was it had more streets, less deaths per capita and more dang cats than a guy could shake a stick at. It was said the town dads liked to brag at each other this model community was hub of the universe. While essentially a cow town it catered to tastes and diversified interests far in excess of those to be found at Pierce, Dos Cabezas or Benson. Though not as cosmopolitan as Tombstone it had nearly as large a number of oases and, surprisingly, only one church. Which dispensation suited Travers admirably.

Stepping into the first deadfall he came to he wet his whistle with beer from the tap while he buttonholed a poker-faced barkeep.

"Hands? What kind of hands are you lookin for, Mack?"

"Kind that work cattle and don't give a rap whose brutes they push."

The apron, thoughtful, took a good look around before lowering his voice with the desired information. Travers slipped him a tenspot and the barkeep said, "Jest ask fer Wimpy Sellers."

Outside, alert, Travers got on his horse and moved along the main drag at a leisurely sleepy eyed walk, stopping in due course before the place he'd been advised to try. In outside appearance it looked very little different from most of the other saloons he'd passed. The striking difference inside had nothing to do with the shape or arrangements, the price or the sounds; it lay with the custom, a rough looking lot.

A few sat at tables; the biggest of these had a poker game going. For the time of day there were probably more at the bar than the other establishments about town could boast. Travers, sidling into a hole, rang a double eagle beside an empty glass, inviting the apron to "Set 'em up on me."

Most of the talk fell away. All along the railed side of the mahogany heads twisted to present a shifting line of hard-eyed faces at which Travers smiled, coolly inscrutable as a frog hunting flies.

"Hold it," growled a beefy weather-coarsened countenance three shapes down as the bardog reached for the private stock. "I'm a guy that likes to know who the hell he drinks with. An' that goes double for pushy Johnny-come-latelies!"

With an eye half shut he peered belligerently at Travers.

An immensity of silence pregnantly gripped the smoky room. Travers smiled, unblinking. A darker color crept out of the other man's collar and his chin came up to show peeled teeth. "You smell to me like a damned John Law!"

Men fell back as he came down the bar with his bullypuss scowl, shooting out a hand to slap back Travers' coat. But the hand never made it. Tipped forward with the snarl plainly plastered to his teeth the angry belligerent froze, stiffly still, with the snout of Travers' pistol deeply shoved in the bulge of his waistline.

Travers' smile spread a little. "Go ahead if you feel up to it."

A man can be tough and stay a long way from crazy. This one didn't move so much as a breath while his face turned dark with frustrated rage. Satisfied finally, Travers stepped back, the gun disappearing too fast for eyes to follow.

Somebody drew a shaky breath but it wasn't the fellow

n front of him. "You've got more gall than Phineas
'eel"

"Find us a table," Travers said, and signaled the
barkeep for a bottle and glasses which he carried himself as the burly man with mouth tight shut wheeled
away through the crowd.

He found them a table against the back wall, well
removed from those nearest, and it was plain he hadn't
forgotten a thing. When they were seated Travers soberly poured. "I was told to get hold of Wimpy Sellers.
You reckon he's around?"

The man stared back at him with measuring eyes.
He took up his glass and belted his throat with a good
solid slug, then pushed the glass away. He measured
Travers again. "What you want with him?"

"Got a job that can use a few tough hands. Ever
hear of Star Cross or Ballard or McCartrey?"

The man's eyes narrowed. He poured himself another
drink with those mean little eyes never leaving Travers'
face. "What about 'em?"

"Right now, I hear, they're hard up for water. Nearest
available source is a springfed lake on a greasy-sack
spread that has about a hundred cows registered
Crescent, owner of record an old codger named Lucey,
content to live off his increase. McCartrey and his boss
have a plan going to gobble."

"So where do you come in?"

"Lake is patented. I own half of it."

The burly man turned this over. "So you're huntin'
fer help," he said, with one eye half shut.

"Competent help. I'm not hiring an army. Three
tough hands had ought to be ample."

"Three tough hands with blue whistlers through 'em
is three little dead men in case you ain't noticed."

Their eyes locked hard. "I pay well," Travers mentioned. "But it's your choice, friend. If it sounds too
rough I'll get hold of Sellers."

"You've got hold of him now."

"Then maybe I've been sold a short bill of goods." Sellers growled. "Who put you onto me?"

"What difference does that make? I was given to understand you were a pretty tough chicken. Someone clipped your wings?"

The burly man pushed back with a curse. But a wolfish grin crossed his saturnine features when Travers continued to sit coolly watching him. "You've got more gall than a pair of brass monkeys!" He beckoned Travers to a window on the room's far side, rubbed a place clean on the fly grimed glass and pointed.

Travers, not too keen about splitting his attention, put an eye to the pane to find the view blocked by the trunk of a cottonwood. The tree was three feet across and sprang in the middle of the side toward the street was one of those likenesses they'd got out at Ehrenberg. REWARD—$2500.

"Poco dinero," he observed, turning back, more than half expecting to find a gun in Sellers' fist. "Maybe you missed a bet just now."

The burly man grinned. "I look like a bounty hunter?"

"That brand of scalper comes in all shapes and sizes. I take it, then, you figure this frolic could be right up your alley."

Sellers' grin deepened. "Remains to be seen. How big is well?"

"Would twenty-five hundred and no questions suit you?"

Sellers' glance curled around him. "By the week or month?"

"By the job," Travers said. "You to pick up two more and pay them out of it."

"Well, now . . . that the best you can do?"

"For that kind of money I could hire half of Willcox."

"You wouldn't git much if you hired the whole burg."

Travers said, unblinking, "It's your move, friend."

"Don't push me, bucko."

But Sellers' look didn't match the ugly sound in his voice. There was guile in his stare and Travers wrote himself a note to keep this fact well in mind.

"You couldn't make that an even three grand?"

"I don't intend to," Travers said. "You'll find plenty of ways to make yourself a bonus. Just make god-awful sure you don't try to cross me up."

Sellers chuckled. "Guess that could turn out pretty painful."

"You better believe it." Travers grinned, too.

The burly hardcase reached for the bottle. "Okay, bucko. You've got yourself some hands. When do we show?"

"Tomorrow." Travers, digging a roll from his pocket, counted onto the table seven crisp hundreds and five used tens. "You'll come into the rest when the job is done. Shouldn't take over two weeks . . . with luck. And there'll be just one boss in this little caper. Crescent ramrod—me, to be explicit."

Travers didn't immediately set out to get home. After quitting Sellers—throwing a look both ways—he stepped back to that tree and tore off the dodger which he grimly crumpled and thrust into a pants pocket. There were probably others and this plagued him considerably but only a fool would mosey round looking for them.

Getting into his saddle he cut across to Dos Cabezas, where he set up some cans to demonstrate his talents. A crowd grew around him as the racket attracted attention. He called for some bottles and when he'd broken those he blew the smoke from his pistol and, looking over those present, asked if anyone figured to beat that.

He got just one taker, a pimply faced kid in a calfskin vest. Travers eyed him disparagingly. "What's it worth?" the kid asked.

39

"Drinks all around."

The kid said cockily, "Will you make good for every dollar I bust?"

Travers, thinly smiling, nodded.

Almost before he could step out of the way five silver discs whirled above the kid's head. A pistol whipped into his left fist spewed flame in a sharp rolling burst of exploding sound. Two of the five coins came down unscathed and the kid, picking them up, slanched Travers a grin.

Travers pulled his stare from the smoking weapon and got three cartwheels out of his pocket while the crowd whooped and hollered. "Where's them drinks?" a seedy oldster called and Travers paid up, still watching the kid.

"You made one bad mistake. If I'd come here to put you out of your misery you'd have been at my mercy with an empty fist."

Below the challenging eyes the kid showed him a sneer. "How much you got says so, Pop?"

Travers, silent, slipped a bill from his roll; crumpling it into a ball snapped it toward the kid's feet. As it left his fingers the kid's gun banged again. The bill disappeared.

Travers said, ignoring the crowd, "Your folks should of paddled you more when you was little."

"Ain't got no folks."

"You want a job with me?"

"Shootin' job?"

Travers, eyeing him distastefully and not much liking what he saw in this kid, reluctantly agreed. "It might come to that."

"I'll take it."

Travers stared a while longer, sorely tempted to leave the whole thing right there. But he was under pressure from the guile he had glimpsed in that twisty hardcase he'd hired over at Willcox. "Go fetch your horse and any possibles you're needing. I'll wait up for you on the road to Bowie."

VII

WHERE THE Bowie trail left the road from Willcox to cross the Cherrycows through Apache Pass Travers reined his mount into a clump of cedars and got down to rest his butt in their shade. He was too experienced to feel very happy.

He tried to view the day's accomplishments as gains far exceeding anything he could reasonably have expected but his judgment wouldn't hold still for that.

So he'd hired some tough hands, but he too well knew that anyone who takes this road leaves himself wide open to at least as much trouble as he hopes to give others. Fighting fire with fire can be a heap precarious and paying men lavishly buys nothing but contempt. What trust could you put in a feller like Sellers? That kind of ridgerunning rogue, should it suit him, would have no compunctions about swapping sides or even turning Travers in for the twenty-five hundred Kohler's kin had put up.

Travers couldn't convince himself he'd had no other choice. No one had stuck a gun to his head to force him into this crazy fix; it had never entered Kate Ballard's mind to suggest he buy himself a piece of Crescent. Chances were she wouldn't even like it—yet how else could a man keep a pigheaded nump like Lucey afloat? What help can you give a fool who won't help himself?

He'd had to put himself in the driver's seat and the

quickest way was to become a part owner—and no two men, no matter how determined, could expect to hold off an outfit like Star Cross. So he'd had to hire help, and a big crew wasn't the answer.

He looked Sellers over in his mind once again and couldn't feel any better even while knowing he needed that kind of help. And because he couldn't trust him he had taken on a gun quick kid that put knots in his stomach every time he thought about it.

Leaning against his unlovely roan he dug the crumpled dodger from his pocket and set fire to it, dropping it when the flame reached his fingers, stomping the ashes into the gravelly ground. He knew what he ought to do was ride clean out of this country quick; at the same time he understood he wasn't about to give in to this.

There were things in his past he was not too proud of but that Ehrenberg business wasn't among them. He hadn't killed that damn fool! All he had done was take fifty thousand away from him at riverboat poker, never guessing the game was rigged till he'd seen the bastard dealing from the bottom of the deck.

But this was no time to be mulling that over.

It wasn't yet too late to leave that kid out of this. He'd be a worse responsibility than a basket of snakes —you could tell he was unstable just from the look of him.

Travers, grunting, swung aboard his horse.

A very healthy notion but somewhat tardy reaching him, for as the roan forced his way through the scratch of branches the kid turned off the Willcox road. They discovered each other at about the same instant.

"You got a name?" Travers asked when the kid came up.

"Bronc Reider." There seemed a kind of defiance to the curl of his lip but Travers kept his thoughts to himself.

42

"All right," he said. "Come along," and kneed his roan toward the road the kid had just been traveling.

Reider, scowling, held his place. "Thought we was headed for Bowie."

"I know," Travers said. "I trust your friends think so."

"Ain't got no friends."

A man could understand that but Travers didn't see that it would help to say so. He continued to move his horse toward the road and before very long heard the kid spurring after him. "Hey! Where we goin'?"

"If you take the job—"

"Hell, I've already took it."

"Yeah," Travers said, and relapsed into silence through five miles of foothills that steadily climbed toward the frowning ramparts of the sun-streaked Cherrycows, trying to think how this trail had looked yesterday from Crescent. When he found what he wanted he cut off to the left, Reider, sullen and resentful, stubbornly clinging to his wake and feeling, by the look, more put upon every moment.

When Travers presently paused to blow the horses Reider said, "When'd you have a good drink last?"

It fetched Travers' head around. That was cutting pretty close. Close enough, anyway, to make a man wonder. Such discernment scarcely fit the picture shaped by other increments or the willful heat so brightly burnishing his stare.

But wasn't that the way it always had been with people? Soon as you packed them into some niche they developed contradictions.

So this kid wasn't quite so puking dumb as he had thought. That didn't change the rest of him, the sallow savagery about him which had first caught Travers' notice.

He considered the bony features, the pimply skin spread so thinly over them it looked like sweated

43

parfleche. He was sure he had this kid pegged right. "So what's your beef?" he said to him curtly.

"There's somethin' fishy about this. I wanta know what I been hired for."

"Chore boy."

Reider's stare looked like two gangrenous holes in the livid features that peered with fierce fury from under the cuffed-back brim of his hat.

"Don't get your steam up till you find you've got something to get in a boil about," Travers drawled. "You asked what you were hired for and that's what we'll tell 'em. Your real job is watchdog. Because there's like to be fireworks I've hired myself a trio of ridgerunners. They have their uses, all right, but a man never knows where he's at with that kind. So I've hired you to watch them. Ever hear of Wimpy Sellers?"

Reider, swallowing uncomfortably, shook his head.

"He's the pick of the lot, a typical no-good that fancies himself to be a smarter Clay Allison. He's the one I want watched." Travers eyed him a moment. "There's a girl on the place. You stay away from her. Savvy?"

Spots of color appeared on Reider's tight cheeks and the green eyes he lifted stared unblinking as a cat's. The grunt he managed might have meant anything. Travers didn't press it. "She's the daughter of my partner, Old Man Pete Lucey. She acts kind of loco—damn near shot me yesterday. I don't want no trouble with her old man over her. You'll chore for the outfit but take your orders from me."

The kid got the makings from his shirt and built a smoke. "You ain't said yet what I git out of it."

"That remains to be seen. You'll draw fifteen a month from the books plus five hundred cash bonus when I take you off Sellers, or when friend Wimpy ceases to be a liability. You'll do exactly what I say or I'll run

44

our ass off Crescent." He peered around. "Now let's
get up there."

There was no trail into Crescent from this direction
but with the landmarks firm in mind Travers had no
trouble finding his way up the brush clad slopes. The
sun dipped down behind the higher crags and the growls
from Travers' stomach told him time was getting on.
Without extending their mounts, and the terrain didn't
favor it, they'd do well to make the ranch in time to
fasten on the nosebags.

The going was rough. Time and again they were
forced to find a way around scaly outcrops of rotten
frost-cracked ledgerock and innumerable house-size
boulders exposed by wind and weather. The horses
didn't care for this climb and had continually to be
prodded. There were places where Travers and Reider
had to get clean off and lead them, but the kid with
unexpected fortitude kept his opinions behind clamped
teeth. Once while they were resting he wanted to know,
since there was one old man already on Crescent, what
he was supposed to call his employer.

Travers gave him a sharp look. "Boss'll do. If you've
got to have a handle you can call me Johnny."

The kid's cheeks showed no change but there was a
skeptical look to the cut of his eyes that fanned Travers'
nerves like the screech of a saw. Reider might wonder
at being handed a first name; it was unlikely, however, that he would have any reason to suspect a partnership rancher of being other than he seemed.

VIII

LAMPLIGHT GLEAMED, butter yellow, from the house
shack's propped-open windows when they came in sight
of Crescent's night filled yard.

Though he had not thought to find a hoedown in progress, the close-packed stillness neck deep about the place stuck a jarring chord at the back of Travers' thinking, bringing him stiff-legged upright in the roan's boxed stirrups. Stopping the horse, he pushed a hand out, eyes digging into the blue-black shadows.

Loud beside him was the kid's nervous breathing.

Through the creak and pop of leathers Travers hung Indian still till he made out a huddle of horses just behind the light from the house's open door. "Company," he grunted behind shut teeth, and came out of the saddle. "I'll handle this. You stay with these nags."

A lift of harsh voices burst from the stillness, angered and arrogant in their swift spate of words.

Cat quiet, Travers moved toward the open door knowing from the sounds that they were in the front room. The girl's voice, defiant, went raggedly rocketing through a quick scrape of feet, choked off by the hard strike of flesh against flesh.

Travers held to his pace, empty hands whitely fisted locked in a wildness that called to old hungers. Pausing outside the long splash of light he threw a bleak counting look at the alien horses before striding on to step into the house.

The girl, flushed and bruised, was backed against a table, print of hard knuckles lividly etched across one cheek. Her father, arms twisted painfully behind him, was like a crazed bull in the grip of two strangers. Facing the girl, dominating this scene, stood a moustached man in benchmade boots with black hair and eyes that held a bully's amusement.

He had his back to the yard and was saying, "Tryin' to play smart will only get you hurt. No one's goin' to shrug off six butchered beefs, so why don't you act sensible an' admit your ol' man paid this feller t' kill them?"

46

"With what?" she cried. "He can't even buy me a decent dress!"

The moustached man wasn't going to be put off. "I can spend all night in this dump if I have to." His voice took on a grating snarl. "That son-of-a-bitch was traced to this spread! You want me to take you plumb apart?"

"Leave her alone," Lucey growled. "I shot your damn cows."

"That's better," purred the big shouldered man with the moustache, wheeling to move across the room toward him. But one of his understrappers had glimpsed Travers now and his startled expression spun the boss man around.

The boss' stare winnowed down to glittering slits.

"Go ahead," Travers invited. "Put your paw on that iron if you want to be lugged out of this feet first."

Thumbs idly hooked over a black line of belt Travers watched all three of them, inscrutably unreadable. "You that's been doing all the yapping—you got a handle? Travers asked.

"Deke McCartrey. I'm—"

"Thought maybe it was *Skunk*. You sure I'm not right?"

McCartrey's tongue licked across his lips.

"All right, Skunk. Since you feel like beating up someone try me."

The other pair had let go of Lucey but nobody rushed to call Travers' challenge.

"You'll never get a better chance," Travers taunted, and pinned McCartrey with a mocking stare. "I'm the son-of-a-bitch you been talking about—ain't three to one good enough odds for you?"

When nobody moved he showed his contempt by removing his stare to swing a look at the girl. "Give him back that slap. Maybe he'll try to grab up his gun."

"Keep away from him, Pita!" her old man growled.

47

Travers laughed shortly and stepped clear of the door. "If you sports got no further business you better climb on your nags and build a shuck out of here. Oh, yes—" he said as McCartrey started to leave. "Guess you better know I've bought into Crescent."

He watched this unwelcome knowledge sink in, blandly enjoying the bristling Star Cross boss' scarcely bridled reaction.

But when McCartrey hung onto his ragged temper Travers turned, disgusted, as though to see about the girl. And wheeled clean around to catch both understrappers clawing for their equalizers.

First gun clear spoke from Travers' fist.

Nearest of the pair, yelling, clutching at an elbow, was flung halfway around. His companion, scared witless, let go of his artillery as though the thing had bitten him to throw both paws full length above his head.

"You've smashed his arm!"

McCartrey's eyes were bright with hate but showed no sign of being about to test his luck. Travers put away his pistol with a mocking smile.

"All right. I expect we understand each other. Get that varmint onto his horse, and here's a tip you can take along with him. Any Star Cross gazebo caught hereafter on this range for whatever purpose—including homesteaders—better shoot on sight. He won't be apt to get any second chance."

As soon as they were gone Lupita cried at Travers in a shaken voice: "You tricked those punchers into going for—"

"Of course I did," Travers told her bluntly. "An object lesson was plumb overdue—I'm only sorry it wasn't McCartrey." He looked at her father. "Let's get into what brought them over here. You must of been out of your school teaching mind to think you could butcher six—"

48

"I never—"

"Goddam it! I heard you admit . . ."

Lucey said, scowling, "I had to get them off Pita. You think I'm plain crazy? Go look around. If you find any shot steers I'll eat them, hooves, hide and horns!"

"You're asking me to think they just made that up?"

"Last steer I killed was two months ago. If they didn't make it up they must have killed them themselves. There's no dead cows at this end of the range."

"So maybe," Travers said thoughtfully, "they just wanted an excuse to get tough with you people."

"McCartrey's pestered us before," the old man said, and shut his mouth ill-humoredly when he observed Travers eyeing Lupita's flushed cheeks.

"They've pulled out," Reider said from the open door.

Both Luceys spun round, the old man diving for the wounded puncher's forgotten pistol. "Take it easy," Travers grumbled. "This feller's our new chore boy," and performed the introductions. "I've got a crew showing up sometime tomorrow. Tough nuts I hired over at Willcox."

"You'll be paying them then," Old Pete said ungraciously.

"I intend to." Travers nodded. "They'll bed down in that other shack. Your girl can cook—"

The girl said resentfully, "You're pretty damn free!"

"If you don't want to do it—"

"A girl likes at least to be *asked*."

"Miz Lucey, ma'am," Travers said, straight-faced with the disreputable hat clapped against his chest, "will you do this outfit the incalculable honor of presiding over its pots and pans?"

He laughed when she furiously stomped out.

Old Pete threw his hands up. "Women!" he said. "A man can't hardly get along without 'em."

Her father sliced him a wide eyed look that held more of an edge than seemed to be called for. "Sometimes it's hard to know what to do *with* them. I suppose having no mother . . . but she'll do it," he growled, peering round at Reider. "Hadn't you better pack in that grub?"

The kid looked blank. Travers snapped his fingers. "I clean forgot the need for supplies!"

"You can send the boy in with the team. . . ."

Travers shook his head. "Reider'll have plenty to do right here. It will cause less talk if you go yourself."

Lucey's stare was searching. "You wouldn't be trying to get rid of me, would you?"

IX

NEXT MORNING, after Old Man Pete Lucey had driven off, scowling, in a rattletrap wagon behind a razorback mule and a flop-eared horse too fat to work, Travers called out the girl and, putting on his best face, asked if she wouldn't care to show him where Crescent's critters were in the habit of grazing. "Be a favor," he assured her, "and maybe give you a chance to catch a breath of fresh air."

Her stare considered him like a fractious colt's.

Travers grinned. "No need to get the wind up. It'll be quite a strain but I'll behave. Best I'm able. If you're worried about your virtue I guess we could take the kid along."

She tossed her head and with a twist of red lips said, "I'm not afraid of you. Go ahead, get the horses. I'll be ready soon as they are—mine's the freckled gray."

Travers saddled the roan, then took down his rope to catch up the gray which was running in the trap off behind the corrals. Reider came out of retirement to watch him.

While he was saddling the gray the kid said, with thumbs importantly hooked to his gun belt, "I heard what you told them birds last night. If they show up whilst you're gone you want me t' take care of 'em?"

Travers gave him an appraising stare. This galoot could turn out to be quite a nuisance. "I want you to leave them—and everybody else—strictly alone. Even Sellers. You understand? All I hired you to do is watch him—"

"Then how come all that burnt powder yesterday?"

Travers peered irritably. "I wanted to make sure the man I hired could protect himself. I don't want you swaggering around this place like a half-ass gunfighter. You act and look like a chore boy, Reider, or I'll find me someone who can. Is that clear?"

It was plenty apparent this did not sit at all well with the kid, but after a moment his glance swiveled away. "All right," he muttered, sullen faced, "but any-one tries t' throw a gun on me—"

"Nobody's going to if you act your age. Now get that chip off your shoulder and clean out those pens."

He saw Lupita, coming up, throw young Reider a curious glance, but she took the gray's reins and swung up without comment. She had changed to a split riding skirt of scuffed corduroy and topped this off with a shirt of checked gingham that revealed almost as much as it concealed. She noticed his appraisal and grinned at him wickedly. "I trust you'll be able to keep your mind on the scenery."

Travers drew a long breath. "I hope so, too."

He could feel the kid's sour stare reaching after them, spurred by the lord only knew what lascivious notions. But the tumbled hills, thatched here with yellow grass and glimpsed stretches of benchland, soon shook the young hardcase out of his thoughts—or perhaps it was Lupita. Certainly this morning she appeared determined to show the new partner a side of her nature that was wholly enjoyable. She had her best foot forward and in new climate Travers found it hard to keep his guard up against her.

She'd been emotionally starved in this stagnant existence and listened enthralled to his accounts of far places. Her mother, it appeared, had come from Durango and Travers, who had himself spent time in that vicinity, told her of mines and mining men he had known there, encouraged by her interest.

The horses picked their own pace, occasionally taking advantage of their riders' preoccupation to snatch unhurried mouthfuls of the lemon colored grass. The girl said nothing of her loneliness at Crescent, the stark drabness of her life there with nothing but her thoughts and dreams to call upon for nourishment.

Yet plainly Old Pete's daughter was a girl of many faces. Travers was startled when with some abruptness she soberly said, "I've noticed the way you've been peering around as though something you sought wasn't quite where you thought it was. You didn't take off on this ride for my company or come all this way for a look at our cows."

Travers made up his mind. "I did kind of hope to catch a look at those fellers McCartrey was going to put out here to homestead."

"And how did you discover that was what he had in mind?"

Travers chuckled. "You don't miss much, do you?"

"It's a habit you get into when you're bottled up like I've been. I don't need any spectacles to tell myself there's a lot more to you than you'd have people think." She said, with her dark eyes rummaging his face, "I can't believe you just happened to come by here."

"I didn't. I came to warn—"

"Of course," she smiled. "You told us that. But Galahads don't ride ewe-necked roans and Good Samaritans around here are scarcer than teeth in a hen's mouth."

Travers stared at her, silent.

"The kind of men who come through Wildflower generally fall into one of two categories. Mostly saddle bums, footloose drifters. You look the part but you forgot to tailor your language to fit."

"My," Travers said, digging up a grin, "looks like you've been readin' some pretty lurid stuff."

"A person would have to be pretty ignorant to find anything lurid in Scott, Thackeray and canned goods labels. If you were able to discover so much of Ballard's intentions you must also have learned that fetching us word wasn't like to change a thing." She considered him coolly. "With this much established it becomes pretty obvious—"

"Is this what your father thinks?"

"My father keeps his thoughts to himself. It becomes rather obvious," she continued, watching him, "that your story about Star Cross—though it's likely true enough—was only an excuse to look the place over. You had a lot better reason for buying into Crescent and shouldering yourself with other people's troubles."

Travers eyed her with very mixed feelings, alarm taking up quite a lot of his attention. This girl was far shrewder than he'd put her down for and her old man, maybe, was shrewder still. Question now was which way to jump.

"And what," he asked, trying hard to sound skeptical, "was that other category you put strangers in?"

"The kind that are always looking over their shoulders."

He said, glance narrowing, "You think that I—"

"I think you came here to hide. I'm sure of it."

He forced a laugh. "That certainly makes sense. A guy running from something buying into a range war!"

"It wasn't a war till you came along. We were already licked, as you very well know."

She had the kind of eyes that were hard to fool. They told him now that he was wasting his breath but he

53

had to say anyway, "It scarcely adds up that someone trying to hide would go sticking his neck out to prod up trouble with a spread big as Star Cross."

"I expect you counted on that," she said, smiling. "We're not scorning your help—whatever your reasons I'm glad you're here."

And right there's where they left it.

A word to the wise, Travers mused uncomfortably as he followed her silently back to the ranch. Why had she told him these things? What was back of it? Why had she opened her thoughts like an album?

Because she wanted to know. That was obvious enough. But there was bound to be more back of this play than that.

Why did she want him to know? he wondered, and darkly considered the two or three things that leaped quickest to mind. Softly swearing, he went over it again.

Her shrewd guesses, unconfirmed, remained only suspicions. But suspicions were tinder in a climate of this sort. They had marketable value, could snatch the rug right out from under him. Was this what she wanted him to think about?

X

HE HAD other things to catch his attention when they turned into Crescent's weed stubbled yard. There were horses in the day pen and strangers comfortably sprawled on the warped gray planks of the railless front porch.

Travers' searching glance, raked across what he could see of the place, failed to discover either Reider or Old Pete's wagon but had no difficulty recognizing Sellers. The pair he had with him looked cut from the same bolt.

The littlest one rolled to his feet while the other guy whistled and three sets of eyes boldly ogled Lupita. Travers settled his stare on the pug-nosed Sellers as the whistler got leisurely up off his butt.

"Come along," Travers growled. "I'll show you galoots where to put your possibles."

Sellers came felinely onto spread legs, a chessycat grin peeling the lips off his teeth. "Hadn't I oughta know this lady? What's all the rush? Ain't the laborer worthy of his hire no more?"

Travers, hanging onto his temper, said, "My partner's daughter, Miss Lucey. Wimpy Sellers. Mr. Sellers has signed up these people to work for us—he'll be a kind of straw boss . . . in the gun packing department."

Unabashed, Sellers, with one eye half shut, pulled the hat from his ragged thatch of rusty hair to fold the top half of him over his shell belt in a travesty of elegant good manners. With the hat back on his head he approached the girl at a saddle cramped swagger to grin up into her encouraging face. He said, "Don Quickshot, ma'am. Your reliable friend an' humble servant."

"All right, Sellers. You weren't hired to please women. Get the hulls on these horses. I've got things for you to do."

The clowning gunfighter, twisting to throw a testy look across his shoulder, reconsidered in the light of Travers' scowl and grumpily nodded. "I'm comin'—keep your shirt on." He directed another smirky grin at Lupita. "Anythin' you want, ma'am, just sing out an' Wimpy—that's me—will see plumb pronto that you git it."

"I'll remember," she smiled; and he strode after the others.

"Reider!" Travers yelled, pulling up by the bars of the day pen to throw a snaky look at the rabble he'd hired to keep Crescent in business.

The kid, lifting himself out of the shade of the bunk-

55

shack, came shuffling over like the lout he was to peer with a sneer at this collection of hardcases. "Reider," Travers said, introducing him to Sellers, "is the chore boy around here—"

"Hell," Sellers said, putting on to be astonished, "it's lucky you tol' me. With that cannon he's totin' I thought first off it must be John Wesley Hardin!" He broke into a guffaw, happily joined by his apes.

The kid's face got red and mean looking but before he could come apart at the seams Travers curtly told him to go put up Miss Lucey's horse. When he stomped off like a wet cat Travers said to Sellers, "In case that girl should happen to yell to you for something you can send the kid along. He'll take care of anything she needs. I trust I'm getting through to you, mister."

Sellers didn't like it but let it pass.

Travers looked at the other two newcomers. Sellers said in a half angry voice, "That half pint of hogwash goes by the handle of Ringbone Reilly. Other one's Valentine—kind they send t' dearest friends."

Travers said, "Get your gear on them horses. We've got some riding to do."

After they were about ten minutes from the ranch Travers briefed them. "That lake back there and some hundred mixed critters branded Crescent belongs to me and Old Man Pete Lucey. Star Cross wants the water. They've come up with a plan to homestead a couple sections of this grass, figuring to lease and use it as a base for throwing three thousand head on this range.

"It's not going to stop them in the long run probably but your job for the moment is to keep strange riders outside the boundaries I'm going to point out to you. I've told Star Cross ramrod any man caught inside had better grab for his gun."

"Well, that's plain enough," Sellers said, looking round. "What about the local law? We goin' t' buck it?"

A very good question, Travers thought, chewing his cheek. He hadn't noticed any law but of course there'd have to be some kind here. If it ran true to form it would be hand tailored with an eye to future votes. Which was like to leave Crescent plumb out in the cold.

Damned if you didn't and damned if you did! He was beginning to wish he had never got into this.

"We'll try to accommodate it," Travers said, "within reason."

"An' if reason don't cut no parsnips, what then?"

Travers looked at him irritably. "I'm not about to let nobody play me for a sucker. The law, Star Cross, that girl or you."

There wasn't much talk during the rest of the ride, Travers doing the most of it as he pointed out landmarks defining the limits of encroachment Lucey had established for four-legged critters not packing Crescent's brand. And one had only to see these to understand on a free grass range why any man with such notions would never enjoy the esteem of his neighbors. Without wire and no help it was a puzzle to Travers how the old man ever made such a thing stick—even in good times.

He had problems enough without trying to solve that. His own edict to McCartrey, if he was to put any teeth in it, would take care of any spare time he got around to. He wasn't kidding himself that Star Cross wouldn't test it.

Harsh talk wasn't going to hold those buggers back.

"That's the lot," he said presently, pulling up on a knoll for a final look around. "We're wide open. McCartrey and Ballard, with a burnt-out range, no water and no market to unload on for better than glue factory prices, are not going to twiddle their thumbs for long."

57

Sellers said dourly, "I get the feelin' we're headed for a real shootin' fracas."

"If you boys wanted to play drop-the-handkerchief—"

"Oh, we don't mind a little shootin'," Reilly said with a grin. "It's the blood that gives me shudders. All that good red blood goin' t' waste."

Travers, ignoring him, said curtly to Sellers: "You're collecting gun wages. You'll do what you have to do . . . just like me."

"You're the boss," Sellers said.

"I think we'll drop your friends off here. They can kind of cruise around. Any trouble crops up they'll be right on the spot to give back good as sent."

Sellers nodded. "We'll have to git grub to 'em."

"That rock slide we passed. We'll arrange to leave it there. The old man's gone to town for a wagonload. You can fetch some out to them soon as we get back."

This much settled, Travers and Sellers took off for headquarters.

The range was freckled with mile-long shadows when the two men, riding without conversation, crested the last rise and saw Crescent's home place spread out below them.

"Company," Sellers said, nudging Travers' arm.

Travers' narrowed eyes had already discovered the saddled horse standing on dropped reins alongside the porch. There was no sign of Reider or anyone else. Travers used his spurs, Sellers swearing behind him as they raced down the slope kicking dust hat high.

With a part of his mind Travers knew this was loco, rushing pell-mell into what might so easy be a carefully laid trap, yet he was powerless to resist the sudden onslaught of urgency born of a queer disquiet—that unpinpointable foreboding, which had stuck like his shadow through the whole afternoon.

Hauled up in the yard he caught one fleeting, astonished look at the kid—a crumpled heap on the porch planks—as he sprang from the saddle. Then he was in, gun lifted, eyes blazing, transfixed and struck speechless by the tableau before him.

<h1 style="text-align:center">XI</h1>

THE GIRL stood like stone.

Both white knuckled hands gripped the edge of the table, her stare two burnt holes in the look of a face that was gray as scraped bone.

Confronting her, locked in his tracks but head twisting now to discover himself an unmissable target, was the hulking brute that only two days before had flung one man into Wildflower's street and in front of the Mercantile, shortly thereafter, had without by your leave pawed through Travers' belongings.

"Seems like, Marshal, you've come quite a piece for a look at my gun."

The man stood with clamped jaws, eyes unreadable as agate.

"Aren't you somewhat out of your bailiwick?" Travers' voice was flat as the top of a table but a child could have sensed the thin tether of his temper. "Busting into a house, deviling a woman, can be a powerful good way to get some last words said over you."

"I didn't come out here to auger with *you!*" the lawman growled. "What's the *matter* with you people?" His testy glance seesawed between them. "First that numskull outside tries to slip up an' knock the top of my block off. When that don't work you come along an' throw a gun in my back!"

"I guess we been a mite on edge since McCartrey and his bully boys dropped by last night. Perhaps—if you've got any—you'd better state your business."

The marshal looked him up and down. "For a grub-line rider you—"

"It happens," Travers drawled, "I'm half owner of this outfit."

The lawman's eyes bulged a little. "Mean to stand there an' tell me you've married—"

"What's he here for?" Travers asked Lupita.

Their eyes met. Her hands moved aimlessly. She seemed to make an effort to pull herself together. "He says my father's been killed."

Travers' mouth tightened.

The marshal said, with Travers' gaze boring into him, "He stepped into the path of some flyin' lead."

"A little present from Star Cross?"

Stare still truculent, the man shook his head. "Nothin' to do with them. It was that damn Fraskens!"

"The yahoo you tossed out of that saloon?"

"That's him. Every time the fool gits likkered up he seems t' figger he's got—"

"*He* killed Lucey?"

"No. Braced this corset drummer, Bedders. They was on the street out in front of the Mercantile. Fraskens wouldn't really hurt nobody—just tryin' to show what a tough nut he is. Bedders didn't know that. When them bullets started kickin' grit round his shoes Bedders panicked. He shook his derringer out of his sleeve an' emptied both barrels. Lucey'd just come from the store. Had his arms full of bundles. Caught the whole works—walked right into it."

You couldn't tell from Travers' face how much of this he was buying. His stare watched the marshal with no more expression than you'd find on a gate post.

"Don't believe I caught your name," he said finally.

"Hoffsteader."

"And that's how it was, eh? Killed on your street. In broad daylight."

"Dead," Hoffsteader nodded, "before he hit the

60

ground." He swallowed uncomfortably. "Somebody had to come tell Miz Lupita."

"You got the both of them in jail?"

"You tryin' t' make out I don't know my duty? Course they're in—"

"All right. I'll ride in with you," Travers said, and dropped the gun in his pocket. He jerked his chin in the direction of the door, Sellers stepping out of the way to let them by. "Keep an eye on the place," Travers said, wheeling after him.

They were halfway to Wildflower before either man said anything more. It was Hoffsteader then who said, dryly thoughtful, "Who was that ranny stepped outa the door?"

"Straw boss."

"An' the kid on the porch?"

"Chore boy."

The marshal's thoughtful look deepened. "Round here," he said, "a man don't have t' hunt long t' find trouble. He don't have to work at it."

"I found that out."

"McCartrey now an' again seems t' feel the weight of his job somewhat. I'd guess he was feelin' it pretty strong last night," Hoffsteader mused reflectively, still watching Travers.

Travers didn't rush to grab the forelock of opportunity.

The lawman presently said, "You want to talk about that visit?"

"What's to talk about? He dropped by with a couple of hardcases. Roughed the old man up a little, bullied the girl. When I got there he was griping about some shot Star Cross cattle."

"You shoot 'em?"

"No."

"The old man?"

"He says not."

61

"So what did you do?"

"Told him Star Cross better have their guns in hand next time any of them was found on Crescent."

"So you hired yourself some powder burners."

"I'm not about to be pushed off that lake."

The marshal sighed. "For lack of a nail the shoe was lost."

Travers, eyes front, rode in stony silence.

"That straw boss of yours got a handle?"

"What about it?"

"Handle I'm thinkin' of is Sellers. This guy stay away from trees?"

"What's that supposed to mean?"

"Some folks, I've noticed, has a leanin' that way. Take this jasper, Sellers, now. Hardnosed, husky, free as a bird. You might not think it but for two years now Mister Sellers has been skatin' on some pretty thin ice. Any scenery that includes him seems to turn up short on cattle count."

When Travers looked at him, he said, "Not many outfits would care to have him round."

"A man does what he has to do," Travers said.

"But he doesn't have to hire that kind of help." The marshal stared at him curiously. "Don't you care that a lot of poor fools is like t' git themselves killed?"

"I didn't post the conditions. If you're so filled with the milk of human kindness why aren't you over there talking at Star Cross?"

When the marshal didn't seem to have anything to offer Travers grimly said, "They've rigged up a scheme to plant homesteaders on us. Quick as these galoots have squatted and filed Ballard will lease their grass. You know what he's figuring then? To move in every cow in that brand!"

"You can't hardly know that." The marshal doggedly said, "Suspicions an' facts ain't quite the same thing."

Travers said icily, "*You* can wait to find out. If *I* do that Crescent's finished!"

The lawman rasped a hand across his cheek.

"Don't waste your breath," Travers told him. "If any squatters show up they're going to be run off. If Star Cross shoves three thousand head onto Crescent you can be damn sure someone's going to get killed."

XII

THE MARSHAL, digesting this in silence, said at last, uneasily, "I can't quite see Ballard or even McCartrey . . ."

"You don't have to see anything outside of town."

Hoffsteader, white lipped, shut his mouth. When, somewhat later, they turned their mounts into Wildflower's street, he said grumpily, "If you're right about Ballard's intentions the man's in a bigger bind than I thought. Them Scotchmen must . . . At least, you can't lay Lucey's death at his door. Regrettable accident. I saw the whole thing."

Travers said nothing. When the marshal left to strike off toward his office Travers wheeled the roan after him.

Hoffsteader pulled up. "What now?"

"I want to talk to that pair."

The man peered at him. "What the hell good will that do?" A darker color pushed up from his collar. "You doubtin' my word?"

"You wouldn't be the first crooked marshal I've met."

Half turned in his saddle, the big man's tightened shape looked about to fly off and go up in blue smoke. In the gathering dusk his eyes glowed like polished

63

stones. The release of pent breath was a scarcely heard sound as, settling back on the leather, he kicked his horse up the street.

It wasn't yet full dark but the saloons had their lamps lit and light splashed across thickening shadows in elongated shafts. But Hoffsteader's office was dark when they swung down before it.

The marshal, ignoring him, went up the steps; Travers, not far behind, stopped in the doorway while the man put a match to the lamp on his desk. About to follow, Travers suddenly tensed. Hoffsteader straightened, stood head up and staring. With a snarled imprecation, snatching the keys off a hook, he dived through a barred door leading to the cells.

Travers sprang after him, almost running him down when the big man stopped to ram a key in a lock.

There was only one man on the blanketless bunk and he was tied hand and foot, very thoroughly gagged. He didn't look like a corset salesman. He sure as hell wasn't Fraskens.

Travers stood in black silence while the marshal cut him loose.

It seemed to take forever for the jailer to get his voice back. It took a lot of words to get out his story and then, boiled down, it was worth mighty little.

At around one o'clock he'd stepped across to take on a beer and a couple free sandwiches, had gone along then to the Chinaman's to pick up meals for his prisoners. No, he hadn't unlocked their door. He'd pushed the plates in under it, coffee cups after them. When the pair had eaten he'd collected the dishes and toted them back to the restaurant.

No one, he said, had stopped in to see them. He'd come back, glad to flop at the desk with last week's edition of the Tombstone *Epitaph*; and the next thing he knew here he was, bound and gagged, lying just where they'd found him.

The marshal and Travers exchanged bristling glances, neither of them satisfied, Travers openly suspicious, the lawman putting on the best face he could.

Back in the office, Hoffsteader, sitting at his desk, said, "Probably fell asleep an' too scairt of his job to admit it."

"He could have been drugged. Wouldn't of been no great trick to drop a Finn in that beer."

The marshal scowled. "Who'd want t' do that?"

"I don't know who but the *why's* plain enough. That killing smells louder every time you get nearer it."

Hoffsteader stared. He said, neck reddening, "I tell you I saw it—"

"What difference does that make?" Travers said to him harshly. "We're dealing with a pair who care no more about lives—other people's—than a ranch cook would about weevils in his biscuits! If you had to give an off the cuff opinion about McCartrey what would you come up with?"

The marshal pawed at his face. "By an' large, I guess, I'd have t' say he was a feller you could set your watch by."

"And his job depends on pleasing Ballard—even more, if you want, on pleasing absentee owners. Scots like a profit. Leaving aside this drought, which can be licked by that lake, and the depressed state of the market which five-six weeks on Crescent grass might boost considerably, where's their biggest headache? With Crescent's owners, wouldn't you think?"

Hoffsteader's lips peeled off his teeth. "A marshal's job is t' deal with facts. All the facts I can see after listenin' t' you is you're bound an' determined to git powder burned."

Travers, disgusted, wheeled through the door, tramped down the steps and got onto his horse. Lucey's wagon, without team, stood before the Mercantile, bed plainly empty.

Though he looked around there was no evidence at all of the parcels the old man was alleged to have been toting. Either scavengers had got them or they'd been happily returned to the shelves they'd come off of.

Arriving at the livery, Travers yelled for the hostler. "Guess you must be richer than Croesus," he said when the man, still rubbing his eyes, came out with a lantern. "You go to bed with the chickens?"

"It's an off night, Jack. No worms runnin' round this burg on Thursdays. What can I do you for?"

"You got a Crescent team here?" Travers described them. When the man nodded Travers told him, "I want 'em back on that wagon. Where do I find Ogleby?"

"Home, I reckon. But I can't move them horses. Marshal said—"

"You got a bill of sale for that team?"

The man stepped back in some alarm from Travers' look. "No," he said. "But—"

"Then get 'em hitched up." Travers flipped him a cartwheel. "The marshal's not running Crescent. I am. Savvy?"

The man peered at him stupidly. Travers said, short of temper, "Come on—shake a leg. If that team's not hitched when I get back there'll be a mighty sick hostler around these parts. Now where's he at?"

"Hoffsteader?"

"Ogleby."

The man, looking like he wished he was elsewhere, reluctantly told him where the storekeeper lived.

The house was dark. Travers banged on the door with the butt of his pistol and kept up the racket till a man in a nightcap indignantly opened it. Cutting short his spluttering Travers said, "I've come for those supplies Lucey bought from you this morning."

Ogleby said, "You've come to the wrong place," and tried to shut the door, but Travers' foot was a little

66

oo quick for him. Ogleby's voice shakenly told him,
I don't do business in the middle of the night—"

"You'll do business with me. I'm Lucey's partner.
Throw on a coat and get down there right away or
'll help myself."

The man commenced swearing. "That's not a threat,"
Travers said, "it's a promise," and, pocketing his gun,
got back in the saddle. "I'll give you ten minutes," he
said, and rode off.

It was pushing three in the morning with a cold wind
driving down off the peaks when Travers, with the roan
on lead from the tailgate, wearily drove into Crescent's
dark yard.

He got down stiff-legged, leaving the reins round the
whipstock, and yelled for Sellers. When no response
was forthcoming he yelled again, not caring one bit if
he woke the whole place up.

It was Lupita, with a robe thrown over her night-
clothes, who opened the door to ask what was the
matter. "Ain't nothing the matter. Where's Sellers?" he
growled. "I want to get some of this stuff off the wagon."

Lupita, shivering, clutched the robe tighter. "He's not
here," she said through chattering teeth, as the kid, fully
dressed, came out of the bunkshack. "One of the men
came after him about two hours ago. Sellers got his
horse and rode off with him."

"Somebody got shot," the kid said, eyeing the girl.

XIII

TRAVERS STARED BITTERLY.

Reider explained. "I heard this guy tellin' Wimpy.
Them boys treed a homesteader."

"Who got shot?"

"Squatter," the kid said, gusty with relish. "When they ordered him off the fool went fer his cutter an' knocked down third money—he's deader'n a tubbed mackerel."

"Where?"

"I didn't git that part. Somewheres south of—"

"All right," Travers growled. "Help me get this grub off the wagon." He caught the girl's eye and said, "You can show him where to put what we leave." The door slammed as she went back inside.

"Thought I hired you to keep tabs on that jasper," he said with a hard glance at Reider.

"Sellers? Sure, but I knew you'd expect me to use my noggin. I couldn't figger how to be two places to oncet, an' it was plain as plowed ground after the wiggin' you give me your dead pardner's daughter was more—"

"That girl can look out for herself!" Travers flared.

Reider stared, jaw dropping. "But—"

"Next time," Travers told him, "you stay with that fireball or I'll run your butt hell west an' crooked. Now catch hold and get busy or there won't be a next time."

They had the wagon half emptied when the clomp of nearing hooves pulled Travers out of his angry absorption. Straightened, peering, he watched the horseman take shape at the far edge of light coming out of the cabin.

The kid stopped moving. Travers said, "I'll take care of this," and picked up a rifle from the bed of the wagon. "Sing out!" he called.

"Sellers here," the shape said, and walked his horse toward them. He pulled up and swung down, throwing his reins to the kid.

Travers put up the rifle. "All right. Let's have it."

"Your squatters showed up. First galoot knowed me pulled out soon's we braced him. No argument at all. Other guy was jumpy. Went fer his gun an' the boy had t' drop him. Some down at heels drifter. He won't give you no trouble.

"What did you do with him?"

"He was ridin' a Star Cross bronc. We put him back on an' sent it high tailin'." He cuffed the dust from his clothes. Looked up with a grin. "Figured you'd want 'em t' know we meant business."

Travers stifled a sigh. If what the Ballard girl had told him had any truth at all in it Star Cross wouldn't let this situation stay where it was. "McCartrey won't quit—he'll be beating the woods for some guns of his own. You better get the rest of this grub—" He broke off. "If you know something funny I could use a laugh, too."

Sellers' cat-sly grin matched the timbre of his drawl. "No need t' pack all this stuff over there. Kindness of Star Cross the boys are in clover. Got a wagonful of grub they took off them squatters—not t' mention ammo. We got enough of that t' stand off a army."

"We may have to," Travers said gruffly. "You better figure to be camping right out there with them. I won't be needing you here and the next move we catch could have some real weight behind it. You're spread pretty thin. Better take Reider with you."

"That mangy kid!" Sellers snorted. "What the hell good do you reckon he'd be?"

"You'll have a chance to find out."

Reider, when he came up in answer to Travers' call, looked two times meaner than a new sheared sheep. He'd probably caught every word.

Travers gave him the nod. "You're going with Sellers. Go catch up your horse."

The gun boss scowled. "If I had wanted that kid I'd of asked fer him, bucko."

Travers smiled. "You're not disputing my word, are you, mister?"

Sellers looked to be working up a hardnosed reply

but his eyes slid away when Travers said quietly, "Long as I'm paying for what gets done round here I expect to be calling the turns for this hoedown."

Sellers licked wolfish lips. "You're the boss," he muttered.

"Thank you. Be a kind of good thing for a man to remember. Along with that picture you've got in your head—the one framed by a tree."

Travers' wintry smile could as well have been taken for a threat as for warning. However he took it there could be little doubt from Sellers' guilty start that he had picked up the message. With his pug-nosed face in a surly scowl he wheeled back to his horse where it stood on dropped reins.

"Of course," Travers called as a final word, "a man could always quit if it got under his hide. The graveyards are filled with people who found life a little hard to stomach."

When Sellers had gone—face dark with bottled fury, and the echoes of the kid's pounding horse had faded after him, Travers, having given them something to think about, resumed the task of unloading the wagon. A man was a fool to buy into such a bind, but he was up to his ears in it now.

Each step had seemed logical enough when he took it. Driven by her Puritan conscience the Ballard girl, coming to him for help, had opened a whole new concept for Travers. Pursued by visions of bounty hunters attracted by the tempting reward put up for his apprehension by Kohler's impoverished kin, he had seen in her plea the chance he'd been seeking to throw them off the trail. It had certainly seemed to be worth looking into. His first sight of Crescent had confirmed this notion.

It was far enough removed from regular lanes of travel and, apparently, long established—which was all

70

o the good. The likelihood of trouble with Star Cross had made even more attractive the prospective metamorphosis from fugitive to ranchman. Who would expect a hunted man to turn up here? An advertised murderer caught in the toils of a lopsided feud?

The closest town big enough to boast a newspaper was Tombstone, very nearly ninety miles away. With all the juicy doings of a booming silver camp to report in his once-a-week paper what editor would waste precious space on any backwoods squabble as far removed as Wildflower?

So he'd bought into Old Man Pete Lucey's troubles, hoisting them onto his own shoulders. And that, too, had seemed at the time the smart move, for he had seen straightaway that without he took the reins in his hands the ten thousand dollars he'd sunk into this hideout would never get back to his pocket in this world.

But that visit McCartrey had paid with his tough hands and spurious charges had subtly changed the picture for Travers—or was it McCartrey's backhand slap at Lupita that had hardened his resolve to go all out with this business?

He had told himself he'd been left with no choice but to fight fire with fire or say goodbye to his investment—but he could have pulled out. He could have kissed that ten thousand off and scarcely missed it. But pride was something else. He was, he ruefully realized, a man who could not stand to be pushed; he'd believed too long in an eye for an eye to let himself take the easy way out.

So he'd gone to Willcox and with both eyes open hired for the spread this trio of gunswifts. And then, to keep tabs on them, hired young Reider. And now first blood was daubed on the doorstep, and God only knew where the thing was like to end, before anyone hollered calf rope.

71

The inquest on Old Pete's demise had been scheduled according to Hoffsteader, for straight-up noon; and Travers—not unmindful of the risk of being too much in public places—had arranged to have the interment follow as soon as might be.

Though he was not too happy at the prospect, or particularly pleased to be leaving the home place unguarded, he left word with Lupita to call him at ten and retired to the barn to catch what rest he could

It was ten fifteen when the girl got him up and told him his breakfast was waiting. She sat down with him over a cup of coffee while he put away eggs and grits and the thick slab of beef she had fried along with them. He was a little disquieted by the frank scrutiny with which she watched him put away the meal

"I'll get the horses," he said, pushing back. He had expected as he reached for the door for the girl to say, "What's your hurry?" and she did, but Travers didn't stop to dig up any answers.

She was ready and waiting when he returned with the horses. She said, "You're not married, are you?" and he said: "Heaven forbid!"

Already the new day had warmed up considerably and as they came down through the pines into the bright blaze of sun it became pretty obvious it was going to get hotter. These forty degree changes took some getting used to, but the moisture in Travers' palm was not due entirely to climate. He was too acutely aware of this girl.

When she said after a while, "Do you find me ugly?" Travers shot her a badgered glance. "If you've ever looked into a horse trough," he growled, "you know well as I do the answer to that."

Half an hour later, on the dun sweltering flats, she broke silence again. "Deke McCartrey, before Pa ran him off the place, used to claim I was pretty as a

72

aceful on kings, whatever that is. Don't you ever really look at a woman?"

Travers grunted something unintelligible and kicked his horse to a faster gait.

She stayed right with him, persistent as a gadfly. "Don't you ever get lonesome?"

"Sure."

"You're a hard man to talk to. You got a thing about women or is it the Mexican part of me you don't have no use for?"

There was an edge to her voice now that gave Travers warning. He rasped a hand across his cheek, irritably aware that he'd forgotten to shave. She had looks, all right, enough and to spare.

Afraid to turn her against him with things like they were, he stalled: "I like you first rate, but there's a time for everything, and not knowing this morning what we're like to run into I can't buckle my mind down to dishin' up sweet talk."

The whole look of her brightened, he saw with mixed notions. But just as he was taking a long needed fresh breath his glance—wheeling to find the nearing huddle of Wildflower's weather warped structures blessedly less than short minutes away—picked up something else which drove any respite he'd gained plumb out of him.

Coming away from the town in a thin haze of dust headed arrow-straight toward them was the Star Cross buckboard. No amount of prayers or staring was like to turn the sorrel-topped figure into even the semblance of McCartrey or the outfit's finicky resident manager.

XIV

"Who's that?" Lupita asked in an odd tone of voice, following the sudden still look of him.

Travers' thoughts were too jumbled to dig up an answer in the fragmented seconds of grace yet allowed before the rig pulled alongside in a screech of locked wheels.

A kind of silence shut down as Kate's uncertain stare wavered nervously between them. "Hello," she said rather stupidly, coloring, as Travers belatedly dragged off his hat.

Gruffly, he made reluctant introductions. "Miss Ballard . . . uh, Miss Lucey." The stormy flash of black eyes did not at all improve his outlook. "Fine day, isn't it?" Copiously perspiring he plunged doggedly on, "Looks like you've been—"

"Mr. Travers," Kate said with horrifying brusqueness, splashing roughshod through the flow of these amenities, "you better stay away from town!"

With a flush climbing into the roots of her hair she caught her lip between white teeth, aghast at the sound of her own temerity. Then remembering her manners, she said a bit primly, glance swiveling around to once again take in the weedless charms of the curvaceous Lupita, "The tragic loss of your father must have been a terrible shock."

Travers gulped.

Only a woman could so neatly have managed to point up another's deficiency, he thought, shifting his weight in a squirm of frustration while sparks flew between them.

Lupita's tawny stare fairly glittered with hostility. But

if Kate Ballard noticed she was not deterred from whatever purpose now had her in tow. Cool as butter at the bottom of a well, she went blundering on with a do-gooder's dedicated earnestness as foreign to the side of her Travers had seen as could be imagined. "It was to prevent this sort of thing that I asked Mr. Travers—"

"We've got to go," Travers growled, "if we're to take in that inquest."

On the seat of the buckboard Kate Ballard blinked. Soberly catching and holding his regard she said, "But that's the whole point of my stopping you out here— I was afraid ‘you'd come in. You can't! Don't you understand? Someone else has been killed! My uncle is furious. He believes the man was—would it be *drygulched?*—by hired thugs you've imported. That's what he told Mr. Hoffsteader when they brought the fellow in."

Her anguished stare—so remindful of the beseeching desperation that had propelled him into this mess in the first place—beat against his cheeks like the fluttering wings of a terrified bird.

"My uncle is beside himself—it isn't just this dead homesteader. He's told the marshal and everyone else who would listen that it must have been you that was back of what happened to your partner. He said you probably paid that drummer to get rid of Old Pete!"

Travers swore, and did not think to beg their pardons. "I suppose he'll claim next I'm trying to take over—"

"He already has. He says it's obvious this homesteader—"

"God's gut," Travers snarled. "That fool was no more homesteader than *I* am!"

"You can't prove that. He says the man was killed by your imported thugs because the poor fellow, trying to make ends meet, came to Star Cross with an offer to lease—"

75

"But you know better! You heard this whole business hatched! You know the deal was rigged by McCartrey and Ballard as cover for their plan to take over our water, Kate. All you've got to do is stand up and—"

Her eyes grew big. "I couldn't do that. The man's my *uncle*, Johnny! He paid for my schooling. He's been all the father I've ever known!"

Travers gave her a long bitter look, reined his roan around the rig and sent him pelting toward Wildflower's street; Lupita, red lips curled in a cruel smile, spurred her own horse after him.

"You're going in?" she cried against the wind, eyeing with satisfaction the dogged look on Travers' stony features.

If Travers heard he gave no sign. He swung down at the hitchrack fronting the establishment picked by the marshal for scene of the inquest, tossing his reins across the peeled pole. Travers paused on the walk before the largest honky-tonk in town, caught by the sudden scraping back of chairs, a babel of voices as those assembled began to push through the doors.

Before he could grasp or understand what was happening, the marshal himself, catching hold of Travers' arm, was skillfully maneuvering him clear of the exodus.

"You can have your buryin', Travers, whenever you want it. Coroner's through with the body."

"But I thought—what about that inquest?"

"Inquest's over. Only took ten minutes."

Travers peered narrowly. "What did they come up with?"

Hoffsteader hesitated, dubiously eyeing him. Rasping a hand across his jaw, he testily indicated several lingering townsmen until, muttering resentfully, they moved out of earshot. The marshal blew out his breath. "Sometimes I wisht I'd took to weed bendin'."

"The inquest, Marshal. What was the outcome?"

"They found Old Pete"—he slanched a look at Lupita

76

—"to've been the victim of 'carelessness' . . . and strongly recommended your activities be looked into."

"Mine, eh?" Travers laughed shortly. "That ought to please the powers that be." He found the girl's elbow, stare hard as flint. "You won't have to look behind no bushel to find that Crescent takes care of its own."

The marshal's stare seemed to spread out a little. The sound of boots heavily neared behind Travers, the smell of tobacco smoke pungently encircling him. Wheeling around, Travers faced the grin of McCartrey, some two steps back of an important seeming jasper Travers had not seen before.

The fellow inspected Travers with a hardnosed insolence that he made no pretense of attempting to conceal, the hateful stare contemptuous as it split Travers into bits and pieces, arrogantly ranging from disreputable hat to runover bootheels with their cheap nickel spurs.

"Reckon you'll know me next time we meet?"

The man twisted his cigar stump across yellowed teeth, potbelly tightening below the bulldog jaw. "So you're the galoot that's going to whittle Star Cross down to size," he laughed, and swiveled his look at Hoffsteader. "Ain't it about time you booked this hooligan into a cell?"

Hoffsteader's face showed the sting of the remark, growing flushed and irritated, a shade sullen too. "You fixin' to explain my duty to me now?"

With self-conferred authority the big man said, "It's about time somebody took you in hand, Jason. There's an election coming up this fall, case you've forgotten."

"No danger of that, Mr. Ballard," the marshal said, a short civility in his tone that somewhat narrowed the eyes above the ranchman's florid cheeks.

"Well, a blink's as good as a nod to a blind mule," Ballard mentioned. He turned away with a jerk of the chin for McCartrey, then stopped to look back over his shoulder, stare skewering Travers. "In the interests of

77

peace and goodwill," he said gruffly, "I've put two thousand dollars in escrow which the girl can pick up any time she's a mind to."

Travers bit back the sharp retort that wanted out of him and tightened his grip on Lupita's twisting elbow. He saw the dry phlegm in the marshal's stare, wondering if perhaps he had sold the man short. He jerked him a nod and moved the girl toward their horses.

"Just a minute, Mr. Travers. If you don't mind," Hoffsteader said, "there are one or two things I'd like to find out from you. For instance," he said, "while I can't interfere in what don't happen right here, don't you reckon another look at your hole card's in order? Ballard ain't above bluffin' where he thinks a bluff'll work, but this drought has put his tail in a crack. He can git pretty tough once he makes up his mind to it."

"I can get tough myself if I'm pushed hard enough. I've got an investment in Crescent. I aim to protect it."

"I can hardly commend the way you're going about it—"

"No one asked for your blessing."

"Well, that's a plain truth." He considered Travers dourly. "They've got a twenty-man crew out there at Star Cross and a lot of other muscle it might be you've not noticed. When the going gets rough your hard nuts will start lookin' round for a easier livelihood. Might even go back to their old trade of rustling."

"You trying to tell me something?"

"Might happen you could get into pretty deep water," the marshal said, watching him. "Folks could start askin' what brought you here."

"That's easily answered. One word. McCartrey," Travers said without a qualm. "You been wondering how I knew what that bunch was up to. You can tell any interested parties that McCartrey fetched me into this business to move a couple of 'squatters' off for him.

78

But there's some smells even *I* can't abide. So I put my life savings into Crescent. It's going to take some doing to shake me loose."

XV

IT MADE A FINE, large sound. But deep in the middle of him Travers knew he'd about as much chance of standing off Star Cross as a half thawed snowball would have in the Hot Place. They could swallow him whole and scarcely catch the taste if Ballard decided to get on his high horse.

The interment of Old Man Pete Lucey was short as the tailhold on a bear. It wasn't a funeral, just a plain burying. No more than three persons followed Ogleby's wagon and the six-foot pine box on its rattling ride from town to the treeless hill where the grave diggers stood beside their meager hole. There was Travers, Lucey's daughter and Furskins, the coroner who—because Wildflower did not have a sky pilot—had consented, after Travers had dug out his wallet, to read a few picked-out words from the Bible.

Lupita wore no hat, no wisp of veil to hide a grief she did not feel.

If she felt anything at all, Travers guessed, it was a bored impatience to get the thing done with. Dry-eyed, she stood blankly staring at the hole while the roustabouts who'd dug it helped Ogleby's clerk get the weight off the wagon. The Mercantile's proprietor doubling as undertaker—though he'd sold them the box and put Lucey into it—had pleaded press of business as his excuse for sending a representative. A handful of others, Travers thought, might have come had they not so much feared to put Star Cross in mind of them. Any man who had lived all those years in this country must have left *some* sign of friendship behind him.

A narrow squeeze but they got the box tamped into the grave and the town pair stood by leaning on their shovels while the coroner, Good Book in hand, hurried through the requested passages. *The Lord giveth and He taketh away....*

When the book was snapped shut Ogleby's clerk got back onto his perch and the two roustabouts got busy with their shovels. As the clerk was unfurling his lines from the whipstock, the coroner, not minded to indulge himself in more walking than necessary, scrambled over the wheel and plopped down beside him. Neither of them offered the girl a lift. The clerk cracked his whip and they drove off with alacrity.

"I feel about as popular round here as a displaced skunk at a new house warming," Travers said. "Reckon this shows whose side the town's on."

The girl, wrinkling her nose, said something in Spanish that came out like contempt. Which was all well and good if one had thrown off one's fetters and were eager as she looked to embrace whatever life might have up its sleeve for her.

Travers, watching, could not help a dour face.

He had been over too many hills, he guessed. The bright flash of dark eyes as they came once again into Wildflower's street was not lost on him. The quick appraisals, the bold way her glance kept flying up at him, were earmarks he could read too well.

The girl was blossoming right under his nose, an exotic moth wriggling out of her cocoon. One could glimpse in this emergence the end of an era, nor was Travers deceived into taking the mirage for the dry sands of fact.

The capricious girl who'd walked up that hill had come down plumb grown, a woman fully anxious to

80

come to grips with life, brash with the knowledge of being on her own, breathless to test every one of her endowments.

Finally freed of the last tie that bound her, made independent by that handful of paper he'd paid over to her father and her own stake in Crescent, she was now a person to reckon with; and God only saw what the end of this would be.

He tried to decipher what it would mean in terms of his embroilment with Star Cross, and could only tighten the clamp of grim jaws in this view of disasters too abundant and dire. With the wild passionate blood of Indian forebears, the full lips curving red and provocative across the shine of strong white teeth, she was perceptive, headlong, a vessel filled to brimming. And his thoughts went gloomily down a dark spiral, apprehensively aware of his own earthy clay. He was very much aware of having a tiger by the tail, a girl whose claws would be quick to show her displeasure.

When they came to the horses, Travers said, "You wait here," and reluctantly crossed to climb the Mercantile's steps, not right happy to be leaving her alone but worried, too, lest he be caught short.

"Three boxes of forty-fours," he growled when Ogleby ran out of reasons for ignoring him.

The storekeeper, peering askance, drew an uneasy breath and shook his head. "Sorry. I can't oblige."

"Star Cross cleaned you out?"

"No, sir."

"Welll" said Travers, darkly finding a shelf well-stocked with various makes and calibers of cartridges. "Isn't my money any good at this store?"

Ogleby nervously tugged at his whiskers. "Your money's first-rate but I've got my orders. No shells and no weapons for Star Cross or Crescent."

Travers blew smoke with a bite to his voice. "Governor's edict, I suppose?"

"Mr. Hoffsteader's, sir. Very strict about it, too, he was. You'll get no arms in this town—he's making the rounds right now to be sure of it."

Turning away angrily, Travers rejoined the girl. He swung onto the roan, his face no encouragement for small talk. But the girl was a somebody now. She said, stepping into the saddle, head twisting, "Cat got your tongue?"

Travers, wrapped up in his thoughts, made no answer. "Where are we going?" She leaned out to catch hold of him.

"Home," he said shortly, shaking off her hand.

"But I'm not ready to go home. I've got shopping to do."

The aggravated tone of her voice cut through his absorption. "Well," he said irritably, "you can do it somewhere else. Crescent's spent its last dime in this two-by-four burg."

"Well . . ." She stared unreadably. "What about Tombstone?"

Travers said impatiently, "Use your head, girl! We've no time to be taking long jaunts with Ballard stomping round with a knot in his tail."

Lupita wasn't interested in Ballard's knotted tail. "I've got to get some new duds—"

"That ten thousand burning a hole in your pocket?"

Her chin came up. "All right," he growled, grimacing. "We'll go to Willcox tomorrow—"

"What's the matter with right now?"

"Right now's half gone. Stores would all be closed time we got there. We'll go tomorrow sure. That's soon enough, ain't it?"

He could see she wasn't too pleased with being put off. "Pita, you've gone all your life without ten thousand dollars. Another few hours won't spoil your party, will it? We'll go first thing in the morning."

She settled back in her saddle. "All right," she gave n, and they struck out for home.

It was a mostly silent ride, both of them busied with heir own private thoughts. Travers reckoned the girl vas probably planning what she'd buy or maybe just allygagging along in her head with the visions inspired by her newly realized freedom and the picture of her-elf as half owner of this ragtag outfit.

Travers' own thoughts revolved around his own none oo glamorous prospects. One thing he could count on: Ballard would hit back. No two ways about that. He vas too far committed to lay off now.

It seemed entirely possible he might go ahead and vithout more ado shove his whole herd on Crescent. Egged on by McCartrey who had nothing up for grabs out his job it was conceivable Ballard might get right at it. He could always rig up some kind of a paper to bestow on himself a spurious authority. For all Travers new they might have filed those homestead intentions. t didn't make any difference whether the excuse would tand up—Ballard wouldn't be figuring to go to court about this.

Then there was that marshal catfooting about the raw edges of Travers' dilemma. In his present state of mind t might not take very much to push Hoffsteader into naking unpleasant inquiries. A letter to the sheriff or a U.S. Marshal might stir up enough heat to put the bel-Igerent half of Crescent right out of the cow business.

Travers chewed at his lip. But he kept thinking of Ballard and that bulldog jaw. Hoffsteader was right. Absolutely right. Star Cross, if they dropped the full veight of their power on Crescent, could smash him latter than a last year's leaf. Travers couldn't for the ife of him think how to prevent this.

Some kind of distraction was what he needed. Divide up and conquer. It was almighty plain that, except in a hit-and-run sort of a fracas, no four guys were going

to account for or stand off twenty. In a fort or a rock
pile with a Gatling gun maybe. Not on the ground h
had to fight from. There wasn't a wall on the plac
you couldn't smash your fist through.

If a man had more time it might be possible to pu
that pair at each other's throats, but the death of th
make-believe homesteader had been a pretty sharp sla
in the face to Star Cross prestige. You didn't bluff
whole town or get that big by dropping handkerchief
behind folks. He had only to recall his conversation
with the marshal to know the Star Cross reputation ha
been built on roughshod performance.

Demonstrated ability.

Ballard had to retaliate, straightaway and sharply
or the have-nots around here would climb all ove
him. As with all big spreads, once the bigness wa
established, Star Cross, like enough, had been coasting
on remembrance. But if puny Crescent with that big
pile of water could thumb its nose at Star Cross and
get away with it every cheapjack spread in a hundre
miles would be looking for pickings. Ballard couldn'
ignore this.

Travers' worried uneasiness grew apace. If he coul
get these greasysackers back of him now . . . but wish
ing was good time wasted. Until Crescent had some
thing sizable to offer, these one and two-man outfit
were going to stay plumb away from it.

He didn't have to probe long to realize his greates
asset. Money, of course—that roll he'd taken off Kohler
But he couldn't quite see how to put it to work i
Crescent's behalf. He could hire more hands but ex
panding this feud did not necessarily guarantee victory
Tough hands, as Hoffsteader had cannily suggested, wer
inclined to prove fair-weather friends; when the wind
blew against them they could fade like frost before
Tucson sun.

So where did a guy with his kind of problems take off for from here?

Sure, he could go back to viewing the far sides of hills. He could take off on this roan and run scared like the miserable misfits he had on his payroll. Most of them never looked at the gray trail of tomorrows stretched out ahead across the miles of broken promises till a badge, or some other polecat bitterly set on improving his lot, put a posy in their gunslick hands. They never looked at tomorrow for being too busy looking over their shoulders.

But Travers wanted something better out of life. He dreamed of putting down roots, making a stand for himself—which was one of the reasons, he told himself now, he had sunk a good part of his roll in this outfit. It was only money—easy come, easy go.

The truth was he just didn't fancy running all his life. He saw that running, in the end, was only postponing the inevitable. If he had to he could face up to that charge. But he was not going to stake his golrammed neck on the whim of some dyspeptic circuit riding judge and the pressured conscience of a bunch of Kohler's neighbors without he by God had to!

With all these things on his mind he had not been very much concerned with his surroundings. Looking around now it appeared that they'd been making better time than he'd expected. The prickly pear and yucca of the flats had given way to the barbed gray wands of flame-tipped occatillo, greasewood and thorny cholla and they would soon, he suddenly realized, be up into the juniper and granite.

Somehow they'd got off the wagon road which, all things considered, was just as well, he thought, reminded of Star Cross temper. The girl, discovering his animation, said, "This was one of Pa's shortcuts. Pretty rough, I'll grant, but it does stay clear of Star Cross range and may give us a chance to check on some of our critters. There's a point up here that gives a pretty good view."

The terrain got rougher. The trail, climbing now through a clutter of fallen rock, began to snake its way up the side of a cliff and Travers' disquiet grew unaccountably. He put this down to mountain travel, a thing he had never been overly fond of. Lupita, looking back at him over a shoulder, said, "Don't look like you cotton much to these rocks. It's safe enough. I'll lead the way."

In a storm, he thought, this narrow twisty canyon could be a bugger of a place, all wild sound and rushing water, the towering barefaced walls scarcely thirty feet apart. He didn't like the prospect, and liked it considerably less when the three-foot shelf that served as trail abruptly narrowed to a scant two feet that began to be littered with chunks of stone eroded from the rim.

He took a look over the side at the dry rocks below and felt rebellion in his stomach, a giddy queasiness in his head. He hoped to hell she knew what she was doing. He was more alarmed still when the wall above his shoulder began to belly out as they started around a bend.

"Hadn't we better get down and walk?"

Lupita grinned. "No need to be nervous. It widens again up ahead just a bit."

"But if these horses turn skittish—"

Something streaked the rock wall a hand's breadth from his head and went shrilling off with an eerie whine that was instantly swallowed in the crash of a rifle.

XVI

TRAVERS DIDN'T STOP to count his blessings but, reaching for his rifle, piled out of that saddle like hell wouldn't have him. Everything, seemed like, happened at once. Lupita's horse, rearing, struck his head against the overhang, lost his footing and went, wildly pawing, over the edge just as Travers with the strength of desperation snatched the screaming girl clear and dragged her, white-faced and wordless, back under the belly of the quivering roan.

Crouched there, shaking, half paralyzed with shock, they heard the gone gray hit the rocks below. Travers felt the girl shudder and, mouth too dry for speech, in the cold of sudden sweat prayed the roan would best his terror and stay anchored to dropped reins.

The months of disciplined training he'd put into the horse paid off. You could hear the grunts and snorts of his breathing but he stood like a rock while Travers, gray as stretched parfleche, crawled between his hind legs, then helped the girl out. Another report from the rifle could have put the whole lot of them over the edge.

But the sniper, unaccountably, chose to remain silent. Perhaps he had done all he'd ever intended. He may have read into the girl's scream and that thud everything he had hoped for. Or maybe he just wanted them to think he'd pulled out. It was anybody's guess.

Travers was in no mood to make tests. He told the girl under his breath, "We've gone as far as we're going on this trail," and, considering the horse and the prospect again, grimly shook his head.

He couldn't even be sure there'd been just the one rifle. Hope was no good; the graveyards were filled with any number of hopers. The girl was still huddled with her back against the wall, squeezed as far from the edge as this tiny shelf permitted. With an expulsion of breath Travers sank down beside her with a finger against his lips, unwilling to break the deep quiet of this canyon.

That guy could have gone. He could be waiting with Indian patience for a target. Or for some sound which would resolve any doubts he might have bothering him.

The only safe thing to do—and Travers found this mighty apparent—was to get down off this trail and find some other way of getting back to Crescent—which was fine, far as it went. But there wasn't enough room to get the roan turned around.

He had heard of horses you could turn on a dime but he had never seen one turned in a two-foot space that had a wall on one side and on the other an eighty-foot drop just waiting for him to bump and panic.

After a quarter of an hour of silent fuming, with the roan beginning to paw at the trail, Travers got the girl up. Motioning her out of the way he said quietly, "Back up, Blue."

The horse cocked his ears and, whickering softly, swung his head for a questioning look. One front hoof tentatively lifted and he looked again toward the trusted voice, but the other three feet stayed right where they were. He was on dropped reins and could just as well have been staked to a hairpin. He learned his place too thoroughly to pit his strength against anything attached to his head or mouth. Those watching eyes said, plain as print, *If you want me to move you'll have to unfasten me.*

Under his breath Johnny Travers cursed.

Minutes ago he'd come out of the saddle without stopping to think if there'd be anything under him. The slap of a bullet could do that to you; but to try to crowd past the roan right now with his eyes fully opened to the width of this trail was something nobody but a fool would attempt.

But there was more to it than that. Travers didn't know where the ambusher was. The horse, presumably, was out of his sight but it wasn't a presumption a man cared to bank on—not Travers, anyway. He didn't want any part of playing target for blue whistlers.

But he did want out of here. So bad he could taste it.

There'd been nothing to prove that sniper was alone. If he wasn't his cronies could be deployed and edging round to make sure beyond question they had got the job done.

Abruptly remembering he'd quit the saddle with it, Travers looked for his rifle, forced to conclude it must have gone with Lupita's gray. But better that than himself, he grimaced.

There was just one way he might get the roan moved without losing the animal or providing a target to be shot into dollrags.

Catching hold of his tail, squatting, Travers ran his free hand slowly down a hind leg. "Easy, boy—easy," he murmured nervous reassurance, again wriggling gingerly beneath the dark belly.

If the horse spooked now . . . He shook the thought away and, resuming his soothing patter, placed a careful hand about the roan's left foreleg. Moved it down to the cannon. "Lift," he commanded, exerting outward pressure with the cold sweat breaking through the pores of his skin.

When the hoof came up he replaced it, still murmuring, and knelt there a moment peering through the widened gap, reluctant to relinquish his cover.

But was it any more risky than remaining where he was?

Forgotten segments of his life skittered through Travers' mind like the reforming patterns of glass in a kaleidoscope as, with the horse rock still, he eased his shuddery body between the roan's front legs. Like an old, old man he edgily levered himself upright, clothes scraping against the wall.

No rifle banged. When nothing else happened Travers, weak as a kitten, drew a shaky breath. The horse, softly whickering, nudged Travers' chest with his muzzle.

Travers blew out his breath, caught up the reins and took hold of the bridle. He waved the girl down the trail. "Back up, boy!"

Step by step he urged the big roan down the narrow shelf till they found a place wide enough to turn him around. Then, surprised at her lightness, he boosted the girl up, guiltily liking the feel of her and—possibly because of this—more taciturn than usual as, reins in hand, he struck off toward the dun flats below.

He regretted the loss of time almost as much as the loss of his Winchester. If he had been in any doubt as to how far Star Cross was prepared to go this attempted drygulching would have set him straight. He couldn't be sure about Ballard but McCartrey, at any rate, was playing for keeps.

Pictures of Kate Ballard kept tolling his thinking off into detours. Something kept scratching at the back of his mind but he was unable to claw it out to where he could have a proper look at it; all he could be sure of was a growing disquiet, a need to make contact with somebody someplace. An impression he could not shake or shelve.

In spite of his worries—more probably because of them—he kept his eyes busy and his ears alert for any off-key sounds. Star Cross wasn't the only source of danger in this region. Though he'd hired the man he didn't trust Sellers any farther than he could throw him, nor could he safely put Hoffsteader out of this either. The marshal was capable of a different kind of ambush and Travers was not forgetting which side the man's bread was buttered on. It was hard to believe his badge would go against Ballard.

When they got out of the canyon he swung up behind the girl. He was not at all keen about this arrangement. He wanted to get to the ranch as quickly as might be but there were other things needing his attention as well. He told the girl gruffly, "See if we can't pick up Sellers and those gunslicks."

She twisted around to see his face, but whatever she thought she kept it to herself. Travers tapped the roan for a faster gait. Not a punishing one because he wasn't that foolish, but he didn't want to waste more time than he had to out on these flats while the Star Cross rifle pack cornered high ground.

The wind had come up and he didn't like that for it narrowed too dangerously the range of his hearing. He kept his eyes peeled. He saw scattered jags of Star Cross branded cattle and, as they moved higher into the rolling slopes below Crescent, an occasional critter wearing Lucey's mark, which looked more like two sickle moons squaring off for a dance—what the Mexicans called Quien Sabe. But no horsebackers showed. Not even when they came onto range Crescent's crew was supposed to be patrolling.

Travers' face took on a greasy shine.

He did some hard thinking before curtly telling Lupita, "Head for home."

Threading the wind-buffeted rolls of land through bent-over brush and across waving grass he wished for the view the girl had offered just before that rifle had changed his whole picture of Star Cross intentions. They were cut off here with limited vision in country eminently suited to McCartrey's new tactics. Travers didn't know what he might be riding into—and him without a rifle on a double burdened horse!

91

XVII

THE WIND QUIT suddenly when they were on the last climb and the quiet by contrast was even more unnerving to a man with as much on his mind as Johnny Travers. The gelding's hooves in this hush were too remindful of boots walking over a coffin.

A smell of dead woodsmoke seemed to permeate the air. It was all that was needed to make Travers' day. The harsh look of his face when the girl turned to question confirmed her own fears. "They've burned the house?"

Travers' scowl was answer enough.

He swung off the horse. The failing sun struck a shine from the metal in his hand. "Wait right there," he growled over his shoulder as, throwing her the reins, he started off afoot.

He stopped once to inspect the gun for grit, spun the cylinder and went on. McCartrey, it seemed like, had split his crew, so maybe the sniper had been alone after all. Maybe some of that bunch was dug in here, expecting him to come a-running to put out their pretty bonfire!

He was in a mood to put out something. But he wasn't going to be so stupid as to go charging into another of their traps.

His darting glances probed the terrain. He was looking for anything he could remember that might tell him how near he was to whatever was left of Crescent headquarters when Lupita, at his shoulder, said, "The stage road crosses the rim of this hill. Our layout's just beyond. Along the bottoms. Or was."

"All right," Travers said, hanging onto his temper. "You can trot yourself back now and fetch up my horse."

Chin up, she gave him back look for look. "I didn't come stuffed in anyone's pocket tied with pink ribbons. I've as much right to what's goin' on as you have!"

Travers, frowning reflectively while itching to get on with it, had to concede she had something on her side. She had probably been facing up to grim truths for as long as she could remember. Life with Old Man Pete must have been pretty dreary for a girl as stuffed with life's juices as this one. Recalling the circumstances of their first meeting he said, though still scowling, "It's in my mind Star Cross may be down there waiting to—"

"Give us the coup de grass?"

Travers' white teeth gleamed through the twist of his mouth. "It would be right in line with what I've seen of McCartrey."

"I've as much score to settle with him as—"

"No one's arguing with that," Travers said, "but if you aim to be there to buy out Willcox tomorrow you better be remembering he won't be alone. Be reasonable for once and let me handle this."

Without waiting for any more of her gab he cut sharply left on a tangent designed to fetch him abreast of the rim where a thicket of squatty cedars lifted shaggily tortured branches which he hoped might furnish sufficient concealment to give him the look he wanted.

Rimming out in this scratchy cover he was just in time to see the confounded girl, riding old Blue like she was Queen of the May, go snaking him down the sharp drop to the yard toward a huddle of men standing around with their horses among the smoldering piles of what only this morning had been Crescent headquarters.

He didn't waste good breath swearing, though he felt like it. He struck out down a wash in long slithery strides to get in behind them where the wreck of the corrals lay in up-ended posts. The men were too far away to put handles to them but a pair of those broncs, he felt pretty sure, belonged to Sellers and the kid.

He was right about that. This was Crescent's own crew he saw when, hearing him, they spun half around to fling up leveled rifles, Sellers turning loose of the girl to peer, too.

Travers, eyeing her flushed face, ignoring the rest of them, made a noticeable production of holstering his six-shooter.

"What the hell happened to you?" Sellers rasped.

Travers mopped at his face and looked again at Lupita. "This ranny been bothering you?"

"Now see here—" Sellers snarled, but Travers cut him off.

"No one called for your gab," he remarked.

Sellers' swarthy cheeks darkened. He ripped out an obscenity. Filled with the fury of belittled importance this advertised reminder of Travers' contempt seemed about to crowd him off his rocker. He shouted, "I don't take that guff off nobody!" and reached for his hip.

A strained stillness locked in place the frozen eyed group of partisans around them. This tension perhaps began to leach through the more vulnerable chinks in the gunfighter's bluster. His hand slowed and stopped, spraddle fingered, still empty.

Travers had not moved. "Go on—pull it, you white livered sneak," he said coldly.

A drawn kind of grayness settled into Sellers' look. The glassy stare gave his caliber away. A moment ago he'd been all surging temper, a bow bent with its burden of hate behind that wild face flushed with venom and viciousness. Now all his guts appeared to have turned into fiddle strings.

He stood there like he'd been made of wet parfleche put out in the sun to shrivel and shrink, mouth fallen open, bulging eyes filled with fright.

"Fork your horse," Travers said, "and get out of here."

He turned away in disgust and the girl, remembering another time he had done this, clapped a hand to her mouth as though to stifle a gasp. But he did not spin about and no one else moved until his glance, slapping into Sellers' cohorts, drove them blanching against the barrels of their mounts. "That applies to you, too," he said clear as a whipcrack.

The shorter man, scrambling, made a grab for his saddle but the other—bolder or fired by a more grasping cupidity—cried, "What about the rest of that dinero we got comin'?"

Sellers, scowling now and pushed no doubt by the need to save face, appeared to have got back some of his courage, enough anyway to come out of his trance.

He was starting to step away from his horse when Travers' regard again fastened on him. Travers said, "In case you don't hear good I'll repeat it. Just once. You're finished here, mister, washed up, plumb through—all three of you."

"You made a deal," Sellers charged. "Hobey's right. We got money comin'!"

Travers' lip curled. "You've seen all the money you'll get from me. If you're not off Crescent in a powerful big hurry you'll be almighty likely to stay here permanent."

Sellers' face grew scarlet with rage. He opened his mouth then shut it, still glaring, with enough frustrated force to crack his bad teeth. He flung into his saddle like a scalded cat and all three of them clapped in their gut hooks and went tearing off.

"He'll remember that," Reider said, cuffing his hat back. "They'll lay fer you someplace."

Travers looked at the girl. She had a tight expression around the corners of her mouth but her eyes didn't show any sign of loss so he reckoned she had all her father's money on her; there wasn't enough left of the fire-gutted buildings to even harbor a mouse.

It was pretty apparent what had happened here, he thought, glancing about. Finding no one at home, Ballard's crew, in traditional procedure for this kind of go-round, had put a match to the place. Discovering smoke, Sellers and sidekicks in the groove of old habits had abandoned their posts to find out what was up. All this was obvious. What surprised Travers a little was that McCartrey hadn't waited for them.

It occurred to him that this raid, aside from reducing the Lucey outfit to a brand without a home, just might have been launched as a diversionary tactic while others of the Star Cross crew were moving cattle. But there was nothing he could do about that right now.

They must have figured this burning would put a crimp in his resistance. They couldn't have been more wrong. It only toughened his determination. He was not the kind to run from a flapped blanket.

He'd run from Ehrenberg and that was enough.

He beckoned the kid aside. "I've got a little trip to make. Before this came up I promised Lupita a kind of shopping spree in Willcox tomorrow." He held the kid's eyes. "I'm going to trust you to take her."

When Reider didn't answer, Travers said, "You might as well start now."

"That bunch ran off all—"

"You've still got your horse. You can catch up another." He gripped the boy's shoulder. "Take care of her, Reider."

XVIII

THIS HAD BEEN shaping up bad enough before he'd come into the fire-gutted yard to find that damned gunfighter's hands on Lupita. Now the whole jamboree looked to be coming unstitched, falling apart in bits and pieces.

He'd been going to ask Sellers about Phineas Tee but he reckoned there were other ways of tracking the man down . . . and Reider was right. He was in no position to be turning snakes loose. Sooner or later he was going to have to kill Sellers. It was the only way he would ever get shut of him.

Looking back to make sure he'd put Crescent out of sight, Travers kneed the roan north and shook him into a lope. If Star Cross was gathering cattle he had no time to waste. He had to find Tee and the best place to start was where he'd first heard of him. At Willcox. Like enough at that bar where Sellers had snarled, "You've got more damn gall than Phineas Tee!"

Time was prodding him hard but Travers had been through enough tights before to know how far he'd get afoot in this country. He conserved the roan's strength, alternating his gaits, occasionally blowing him while he studied the night sounds and peered grim-eyed across the moon silvered backtrail.

The growling of his stomach was continual reminder of how long it had been since he'd put food into it and the ache in his temples warned that sleep was overdue. But these things could wait. Star Cross wouldn't.

If they'd kept Crescent under surveillance McCartrey would be thinking he had Travers on the run and be driving all out to consolidate his gains. He could claim the place was abandoned; there'd be nobody there to lift a voice against him.

Travers should have foreseen this and stayed himself or left the girl and Reider there. He simply hadn't been thinking straight. Too many things had been happening too fast, but it was too late now. Once Star Cross got their cows bedded down around that lake there didn't seem much likelihood he'd ever get them out of there. Lupita could go to court with it but Star Cross would have possession and a fight of that kind could drag on forever.

He was tempted to go back but experience assure[d] him no practical good would be derived from such [a] course. If McCartrey had the place staked out hi[s] watcher would have summoned all the help they neede[d] before Travers could return.

Looked like a lost cause whichever way you eyed i[t]

Even if he was able to run the man down where wa[s] the advantage? No matter how tough or cunning Te[d] was only one man and no two men were going to sto[p] Ballard.

There was no guarantee he could interest the fellow[.] Like a dog with a bone Travers kept going over it[,] skinning his teeth back, hackles raised, growling.

If he could talk to the girl . . . but he already kne[w] everything she could tell him. He knew the main sor[e] points about Benny Ballard. Caught by this drought wit[h] too many cattle. Job dependent on showing a profit, h[e] was damn well squeezed between Charybdis and Scylla[.] He couldn't put cows on a fallen market. Only thin[g] that could save him was to move them—quick. The figh[t] didn't have to be carried to Star Cross. Keep his cattl[e] away from Crescent's water and Ballard was finished[.]

It was simple as that.

Travers' twisted grin showed his teeth as he snorted[.]

The solution was simple, but how to carry it out? Al[-] ready considered and passed up was the notion of count[-] ing on help from the other small owners. Travers guesse[d] they would sooner tangle with lions. One thing you coul[d] count on: McCartrey and Ballard, if they went down a[t] all, would take some other people with them. Yo[u] couldn't shut your eyes to that.

Dawn was still an hour away when he came int[o] Willcox and found the town still mostly asleep. Some[-] thing else he hadn't figured on. Saloons wouldn't ope[n] for another four or five hours. Too long to stand around[.]

He picked what looked like the lesser of two evils[.]

Hunted for the marshal's office, found it and, grumbling, crawled from his horse.

A night lamp burned from its perch on a rolltop seen through the window. All that came through the door was a sound like somebody using a crosscut. But a marshal was, after all, a public servant.

Travers knocked. The snores continued. He tried again and kept vigorously at it till a tousle-haired jasper in longhandled underwear crowhopped past the desk pulling on a pair of sailcloth pants. "Door ain't locked —you tryin' t' wake up the dead?"

Travers, pushing it open, stepped inside. Running a hand through his hair the fellow said testily, "Who's been killed now?"

"You the marshal?"

"Think anyone else would be hangin' round here? What the hell do you want?"

"I'm trying to run down Phineas Tee."

The marshal's stare sharpened. "You got company. What's he done now?"

"I don't know that he's done anything. What I want to know is where to get hold of him."

"The law can take care of any hangin' that's needed." The man said abruptly, "Ain't I seen you before?"

"More than likely. I'm a rancher. I buy most of my—"

"Rancher, eh?" Picking a cigar butt up off the desk the marshal fired up, peering curiously at Travers through the blue puffs of smoke. "If you ain't bound for trouble how come you're so interested in locatin' Tee?"

Travers said flatly, "I stopped here to get information, not give it. Let's quit horsing around. Just tell me where he's at—I'll take it from there."

"You don't smell like a sheepman."

Travers, startled, laughed too loud. "I take a bath regular," he joked, dissembling, but the owlish fixity of this lanky man's regard did not encourage a prolonged

99

performance. "You going to tell me where to get ho
of him?"

The marshal, still with that lumpy look on his fac
said, "Might's well, I guess. Last I heard he was campe
in the Cherrycows this side of Paradise." He hooked
hip on the desk. "One thing, though, you'd better r
member—this is cow country, mister. You bring shee
in here there'll be hell to pay."

XIX

Sheep.

By God, Travers thought, *that just might do it!*

Having found a livery he left the roan to be fed an
strode back to a hash house called *THE CHINES
AMERICAN*. They were just opening up. "Steak," l
growled. "Hash browns—plenty of java."

A sheepman! He recalled Sellers' description. If T
was sufficiently militant and had enough of an outfit th
might be the answer. And a whole lot closer than
man could have hoped for.

How spread out was he? It took time to move shee
and for Travers time had just about run out.

Remembering the marshal's peculiar stare reminde
him of the dodger he'd torn off a tree that time he w
here on a hunt for tough guns. Among edgy though
about that loomed the look of Sellers riding out of th
yard. It was deep in his bones he had not seen th
last of them.

He tore into his grub with the consuming intensity
a hard wintered wolf, sloshing it down with deep gul]
of hot Arbuckle. Kate Ballard got someway into h
thinking and he pushed her impatiently out of his min

He had his hands full riding herd on Lupita. He hoped to Christ that kid would use his head.

He felt like Atlas trying to hold up the world, yet in spite of his problems and the needs clawing at him the two girls' faces—pixie smile of the one, the beckoning eyes of the other—wouldn't leave him alone. The painful blushes of Kate Ballard caught up in a conflict of loyalties beyond her depth could not hide the solemn wistfulness or the innate goodness of the things she so richly held for the man who would bring her out of herself.

Travers wondered if he was being too hard on Pita. It was not her fault she'd lived nearer to the earth, that her hungers seemed fiercer, closer to the surface. She had never been taught to dissemble her feelings and that barren existence with her father on Crescent, not to mention the restive heritage of mixed blood, must have been like a prison to one carrying the burden of such ample endowments. Her wants were so apparent, her need for affection such a desperate force when put beside her obvious inexperience, it was like an open invitation.

How else could he have handled Sellers? The man had no more conscience than a rutting bull.

Someone had come into this place while Travers had been putting away his food. He became conscious now of that someone's inspection, the feeling of eyes boring into his back, and he wondered if the marshal had followed him here.

He went on with his eating, not looking around. He downed two extra cups of coffee, threw some change on the table and abruptly got up. He scooped his hat off the floor, eyes swiveling around as he straightened.

There were two other customers, the nearer one busily eating, the other by the door with his face folded over a paper. Travers dismissed the eater as an innocuous townsman. The other's face was wrapped around a wad of cut plug and looked entirely compatible to the dusty woollen shirt, greasy calfskin vest and scuffed shotgun chaps.

As Travers reached for the door the hard looking customer lifted pale eyes off his paper to say, "Don' know where a feller could git a job, do you?"

Travers said, pausing, "What kind of job?"

"Man in my shape can't be too particular." He showed broken snags of yellowed teeth in a grin.

Travers considered. "Got a horse?"

"Right outside."

"All right," Travers said, "I'll meet you there in about ten minutes," ducked his head and went out.

A thoughtful scowl was still on his cheeks when he turned in at the livery to pick up the roan. It had nothing to do with the man's rough appearance. Travers described him to the hostler but the man shook his head. "Never seen him."

Hunches Travers could put some belief in, but what sort of hunch had propelled this hardcase into that hash house on Travers' heels or prompted him with what was almost a leer to hit up a total stranger for the kind of work his remarks had suggested?

It looked too fortuitous—too goddam pat. Any man's life rubbed elbows with coincidence. But Travers was sure he'd never seen this bird before. What had given him the notion Travers was in the market? And for that kind of talent! His advent so close to the talk with the marshal was mighty near as unsettling as the ambush attempt.

Travers, leaving the restaurant, had made it a point to catch a look at the horse. Its FS brand was as much of a stranger to him as its rider. There'd been no gun weighing down his hip yet the odor of guns had been unmistakable. He could think what he wanted but Travers, caught up in a welter of suspicions, had not

ired him on account of Star Cross but to know where
e was and to keep an eye on him.

When he picked him up he said, "What do I call
ou?"

There was no hesitation. "Fek Shinnan'll do."

"What part of the country is home to you, Shinnan?"

"Any place I hang my hat. What part's home t' you?"

"I'm half owner of Crescent. At the foot of the Cherry-
ows. Where's your possibles?"

Shinnan said with a grin, "I travel light."

Travers chewed on that till they raised Dos Cabezas.
hen he said, slanchways watching, "Pays a hundred a
nonth."

The new man said just as casual, "You must be
n some kinda trouble."

Travers shrugged and Shinnan, looping brown spit
bove a leather clad knee, observed, "Man don't pay
ightin' wages unless."

"We've got a drought in this country. Sharp auger like
ou must've read the signs." Stripped to essentials
Travers filled the man in on Crescent's present position.

"It's a bastard," Shinnan said. "What you gonna do?"

"What would you suggest?"

Shinnan appeared to give some thought to the matter.
What about dynamite?"

"You mean stampede their cows?"

Shinnan said, grinning through the snags of his teeth,
Might be worth tryin'. I was thinkin' about the lake."

"Sounds pretty drastic."

"Hurt them buggars a heap more'n it would you."

Travers had to go along with that. Practically speak-
ng it made a kind of hard sense. Ballard's cows wouldn't
ake on very much tallow stomping around a blown-up
ank. Shinnan said, "You could build it back later."

With the town well behind them Travers said sourly,
Any other ideas scratching round in your craw?"

"You could hand 'em back a dose of their own. Fire

103

Star Cross. Shoot up their line camps. Hit 'em lik Quantrill lambasted the border states. They're a lo more vulnerable, man, than you are."

"And bring in the law?"

"Law's spread pretty thin in these parts by the looks You ain't got a heap of choice if you figger t' stay i business. How many hands you got we kin count on?

"Toss-up now if I still got any."

Shinnan said, scowling, "You are in a bad way. Wha about this partner?"

"Partner's a girl."

Shinnan scrinched up his eyes. "You better blow u that lake an' head fer timber."

XX

It was noticeable, though, he didn't ask for mor money or talk about quitting. This guy sure as hell wa no ordinary drifter.

As they were climbing into the footslopes he saic "How'd you come t' have a girl fer a partner?"

"In business with her father. He got shot."

Shinnan puckered up his mouth. "What happened t the shooter?"

"Marshal put him in jail. Broke jail and flew th country."

Shinnan pawed at his face. "You've had your shar of luck, all right." He said offhandedly, wholly casua "What do I call you?"

Travers felt a cold wind drift across both shoulder A dozen notions whirled through his head, but, "Th name," he said, "is Johnny Travers," and braced him self.

The new man's eyes were unreadable.

At around two thirty they came onto Crescent range and Travers, pointing out landmarks, told Shinnan about the three ridge runners he'd unloaded. "Sellers," he remarked, "may have a bone in his craw. I think he left figuring he had twice as much coming as he managed to wind up with."

This pulled a look out of Shinnan but he let the words pass. A hard one to peg, forking his saddle like a sack of wet meal, legs hanging loose and straight down as an Indian's. There was something disconcerting about so hard-faced a fellow jogging along without a gun hung onto him.

The feel of hard eyes began to prickle Travers' skin but never when he looked could he catch Shinnan at it. More times than he'd have wanted to own up to he found himself considering the rubber butted rifle slung under this new man's leg. A Henry repeater, favored tool of bushwhackers.

There was a cold malevolence about this hombre, indefinable but plainly felt as the aura of repulsion intangibly attributed to public executioners, and it crossed Travers' mind this son of a bitch might be here on behalf of Star Cross & Company.

He tried to throw off this crawly feeling of edginess. When they left Crescent range traveling into higher country he could sense the man's aroused curiosity but nothing came out of him. Pausing to blow the horses half an hour later, the fellow stayed wrapped in his Indian silence and Travers, rubbed raw, was forced into speech.

"Case you're wonderin'," he said, "we're looking for a jasper known as Phineas Tee," and brought his stare about. "That name mean anything to you?"

Shinnan shook his head. "Nope. What's he do?"

"You'll see when we find him," Travers grunted, and pushed on.

This looked like good country to damn well get lost in, great up-and-down slabs of granite below skimpy patches of bright and dark greenery that probably were trees but looked more like bushes. Paradise, from what little he'd heard, wasn't much, a town built of boards lugged from Curly Bill's Galeyville when the smelter closed down and the advent of Slaughter chased the owlhooters out of there. Getting your bearings in this jumble of peaks would take more time than a man had to give it.

He shot a look at Fek Shinnan. "Ever heard of a town in these mountains called Paradise?"

To his surprise Shinnan nodded. "It's over on the south slope. Bit west of here someplace. That where this Tee's at?"

"I hope not," Travers growled, and kneed the roan on again, swinging him west when a way opened up. "Supposed to be somewhere this side of it."

"What do we look fer?"

"Sheep," Travers grunted.

"Well, by God!" Shinnan said three or four minutes later. "You sure don't mind swappin' the witch fer the devil."

Travers said irritably, "I don't have much choice. I'm not giving up that lake without a fight."

"Brother!" Shinnan cried. "Why not just stick that gun in your mouth an' pull the trigger? You won't be no deader'n bringin' sheep in will get you."

"Look—" Travers pointed, and Shinnan following his hand saw sheep spread below like a rumpled gray blanket. Barking dogs on the fringes were keeping them bunched, heckling the van to funnel them into the narrow gut of a canyon. Travers' glance leaped ahead to hunt for the exit and so missed the look Shinnan's pale stare whipped at him.

Travers' hand rose again. "They'll rim out over yonder —we'd better get down there."

The canyon debouched on a long grassy slope fenced on three sides by ocher colored cliffs. The drop nearest to them was creviced and cleft by fissures and gaps left by great fallen chunks broken out in times past by the action of weather.

Twice, Travers, leading, was forced to turn back only yards from their goal by impassable slides. Even so they were first in the meadow by almost three minutes, long enough for the man in the calfskin vest to say, "I dunno about this. Mebbe you oughta give a little more thought to it."

Travers' eyes narrowed. "If you don't want to stay hired—"

"It ain't that," Shinnan grumbled, and bit off a new chaw. "It's what we'll do t' that range. Hell, you know what sheep—"

"Old wives' tales! Sure, they'll clean grass down to the roots, maybe tromp out some. But if it comes up again cattle will eat it. They drink after sheep, too— I've seen them. Let's get this out in the open, Shinnan. If you're bucking for higher wages—"

He broke it off, staring past Fek Shinnan to where two men, very competently mounted, had ridden from the canyon packing rifles across their saddlebows. Travers held his place as the pair swept toward them.

Shinnan waited, too, with a livid look sitting high on his cheeks and his eyes bright as snakes. Travers, hand up, palm out, muttered crossly, "You have to look like they've got hydrophobia?"

The pair pulled up some twenty feet away. One was a round faced Indio in crossed bandoliers stuffed and shiny with brass; his companion was white, a bony young Irishman with a wildness of eye that didn't give a damn whether school kept or not. "You guys lost or lookin' for somethin'?"

"Guess we've found what we're looking for," Travers said, watching the sheep spill out across the grass. He

107

brought his stare back. "If you're Phineas Tee I've got a proposition that I hope will interest you."

"A kind of Trojan horse, I guess," the Irishman said with his lip curled back. "So now you can turn them broncs an' get out of here."

Travers bit back a scowl. "Be to your advantage to hear me out."

"I wouldn't trust a cowman if he was hogtied an' branded."

"It won't cost you nothing to listen," Travers argued. "The cowman in this deal is Ballard of Star Cross and you don't have to trust him. I want you to help me put a spoke in his wheel. I'm prepared to pay well for it." He said, "You *are* Tee, aren't you?"

The Irishman nodded and appeared, though skeptical, to be turning it over. "You don't look like you could afford a new shirt," he said with frank scorn. "But most people don't that have trouble with that bunch. What's the bitch? He got your back to the wall?"

"That's right," Travers said. "He's got me over a barrel. You ever hear of Crescent?"

Tee shook his head.

"You must know they've got a drought down there. Between lack of grass and dried-up streams Star Cross and Ballard's job are just about up the spout. They've got three thousand head of cows he's got to move damn pronto."

He mapped out Crescent's location. "As a working cow spread it never was much even before they burnt us out. It controls a lot of grass, though, if we had the men to hold it, and a patented spring-fed lake that Ballard figures to annex—which is where you come in. I want you to put these sheep on the place, and you can do it as a partner or I'll take the entire risk and pay you cash money for as much of this flock as I can cover."

XXI

The SHEEPMAN looked Travers thoughtfully over. "Entire risk, eh? Ain't you bitin' off more'n you can chew?"

"Be my worry, won't it—long as I pay for them?"

Waving the Indian away Tee got down off his horse and, fetching his rifle, came to a stand beside Travers' stirrup, looking up at him skeptically. "You got any idea of the work involved?"

Travers said gruffly that he guessed he could manage.

"By God an' brute force, eh?" The wool grower snorted. "Where's your crew? You'd never get a flock this size off the mountain. You got to have dogs. You can't work sheep from the back of a horse."

"Suppose you let me worry about that," Travers said, reaching inside his shirt to get at his money belt. "How much do you want?"

"Never mind your damned money," Tee growled, scowling up at him. "These sheep are my charges." Gasping for breath he cried in a tone that bordered on outrage, "You think I would sell to a ignorant nump who'd get half of them killed before he ever got started?"

Travers gaped at him.

"Come on," Shinnan said with a surly impatience, "you'll git noplace with this pack of scissorbills!"

Travers, trading glances with the Irishman, ignored him. There were things about Tee he hadn't noticed before. Seen close up the man looked infinitely younger, scarcely more than a boy with the adolescent down still clinging to his cheeks. He was not well, either. In the fierceness of that determined glare he might seem harder than nails, but the gangling shape, flushed face and hollow chest bespoke disease—some inner sickness that was burning him up.

A younger Doc Holliday aching to be killed was the thought in Travers' mind. But, bad lungs or whatever, as owner of these sheep the boy would have to be reckoned with.

While Travers was hunting some way out of this impasse, Tee—perhaps glimpsing the older man's quandary—abruptly grinned. "I won't sell but . . ." He chewed at his lip, eyes narrowly wicked. "Is McCartrey still top screw for that outfit?"

Travers, silent, finally nodded.

"Then I'll pick up the partnership end," Tee said, scowling at something that must have been in his head, and brought his stare back. "Be amusin' to see the look on their faces when they find they've got Phineas Tee for a neighbor. How soon do you want these woollies at your place?"

"Quick as I can get 'em. Sooner, if possible."

"You don't move sheep in no hell of a hurry. I may have some trouble gettin' into your country, but I'll get there. You can bank on it."

He reached up a hand and, as Travers leaned to shake it, said, "If Ballard's ready to move, how do you figure to keep hold of that range?"

"With the sheep," Travers said, "and you for a hole card."

"Yeah—but right now? How you fixed for a crew?"

"Two hands and myself."

Tee's restless glance skewered a look at Fek Shinnan. "Not enough," he said shrewdly, "not if that bunch has sure enough got its back up. I'll send some of my boys along with you."

"Herders!" Shinnan sneered.

"That's right. Sonora Yaquis armed with .45-90s. No one's runnin' over them."

Travers shrugged. Indios. "All right." He shared Shinnan's skepticism but was willing at the moment to settle for anything. McCartrey, counting cartridge flashes, would hardly know straightaway they couldn't hit a barn door. If they could hold Star Cross off till this kid got his sheep there it was as much as Travers could expect.

Tee sent a shout winging over the grass, got back on his horse and rode to meet the Indian that loped across to talk with him. The man spun his mount and, circling wide of the sheep, came back with two others. Tee said, "These boys'll go with you."

They seemed alike as three peas shaken out of the same hull, broad faced, swarthy, thickset hombres in ragged pantalones and open-toed sandals, all packing rifles and crossed belts of cartridges. None of them said anything and Travers, looking them over, grunted.

"All right," he said, "let's go," and they set off.

It was in Travers' nature to take the bull by the horns and, far as he could see, this was what he'd have to do. He couldn't see much hope of having those sheep turn up at Crescent before tomorrow night; and, if Tee ran into trouble, it might take longer. Indians of any kind were a touchy proposition. Brave enough, sure, but inclined to be unpredictable. In a bind, under fire, they seldom showed much relish for teamwork, and he'd no reason to suppose these Indians from Mexico would be any different.

What he had to do was hold back the cattle till he could spread Tee's sheep between Star Cross and Crescent's lake. Cows could be stampeded but Mc-Cartrey would know that, too, and at the first sign of trouble would probably let them go. He might even bring his bully boys on ahead of the cattle. Be harder to watch for, harder to stop. Their first objective after all was to crush opposition and McCartrey, at this, was an old and past master.

All Travers had to throw up against them was himself, young Reider and this untried Fek Shinnan. And Reider might not get back in time. But if he could keep these Yaquis from running out on him and nothing else came apart at the seams they might hold Star Cross off until Tee arrived with the sheep and the rest of his Indios.

A whole heap of ifs any way a man eyed it.

"I dunno," Shinnan said, pushing his horse up beside him. "That's a pile of range to cover—even with the six of us. An' how do you know while we're busy with Star Cross these Injuns won't jump us? I didn't like that kid fer sour apples. He's got a bee in his bonnet."

Travers eyed him, silent.

"Put yourself in his boots. Young, sick, ambitious prob'ly—stuck up here with a bunch of damn woollies. You think he swallers that from choice?"

"You figure I went to him from choice? I considered all that," Travers said, "before we got to him. That was my hole card, the thought he might jump at the chance to get out of here."

"Mebbe," Shinnan growled, "you didn't think far enough."

Travers swiveled a sharp glance at him.

"Why," Shinnan said, "should he settle for half when with any kinda luck he can damn well take over?"

"Take over what?"

"Whatever equity you got in that outfit. Your cows *an'* your range—with Star Cross on our necks we'd play hell tryin' t' stop 'em!"

This conception of the outcome had not crossed Travers' mind. But he could see straightaway it was something to be thought about. Sellers for gall had compared Travers to Tee first time they'd locked glances, and the Irishman certainly was bright enough to grasp the ramifications of the deal he'd been offered. First off he'd looked like turning it down cold. What had caused him to switch, to pick up any part of it? He'd asked about McCartrey—was this what had changed his mind? Some old score he thought to even?

"We'll keep our eyes peeled," Travers said. "At least they'll not catch us sleeping. He could have some grudge he sees a chance to pay off."

Shinnan sniffed and spat over his saddlehorn, dropping back into sour faced silence.

Travers jogged along with his burdensome thoughts, too weary to concentrate long on anything, trying to fight off an increasing tendency to drowse. Several times he found himself about to float off and jerked the chin off his chest in guilty alarm. On one such occasion, pawing the sweat off his face he caught glimpses through boulders of Crescent range spread below and realized with a start they they were on their way down.

So was the sun. In another hour at most it was going to be dark.

Something whipped past his face with the sound of a hornet.

XXII

SOMETHING WHINED off his saddlebow, the wicked jolt of it reaching all through him, the roan rearing onto its hind legs, screaming, as the sharp crack of rifles turned the brooding hush to bedlam.

It was half dark now in the foothills around them, with muzzle lights flashing like Chinese crackers, pitching horses tangled in a welter of confusion as cursing riders tried to keep from being mangled and fight back.

Through the reverberant thunder of .45-90s Travers heard Shinnan's shouts but could not spot the man and found no time to look for him. A riderless horse tore past, hurt and grunting, and a pair of vague shapes suddenly wheeled from the brush in a high yelling racket, the last of these screaming as he pitched with spread arms off the back of his mount. The other kept going, bent low with Travers after him.

Crossing the flat of a talus field Travers glimpsed him again, fading into a patch of stubby second-growth pines that ran down a spur toward the Wildflower road.

The light was poor and getting worse. Night came round like a closing fist. Travers, snarling against the wind in his teeth, called on the roan for all it could give, slamming on through the pines with the dregs of his temper too stirred up for caution.

Whirling out of the trees he found nothing but emptiness and, swearing, drew rein, aware of someone behind him. A horseman materialized lifting a hand—one of the Yaquis. Both held still, listening.

But there were no near sounds, only the rumor of swift fading hoofbeats; Travers, disgusted, would have spun to head back had the Indian not caught hold of his bridle.

"Horse only—no man. Me find," he said, grinning, and slid from his mount to disappear in the shadows, intangible as smoke.

All Travers' weariness seemed abruptly to catch up with him. A faint wind came down off the Cherrycow peaks and he hugged himself, shivering, as night air bit into the jerk of his muscles. He wondered if the kid was back with Lupita and what the end of all this would be. With the reins of both horses he came down from the saddle, filled with the echoing ache of vast loneliness.

Where *would* it all end? Was this the sum total of human endeavor? To scrabble around like a bunch of wild animals!

The face of Kate Ballard, all eyes, came to haunt him, but he knew in his bones their paths lay too far apart. The love of justice they both obviously shared

114

as too slender a thread to bridge the gulf of their ifferences. Even if they both tried.

Girls brought up as she'd been didn't marry drifting ddle bums, and if she would he couldn't let her. He new himself too well. You could teach an old dog ew tricks perhaps but habits that had become a part f him weren't easily pushed aside.

Scrape of a boot on turning gravel snatched him bruptly away from this wistfulness. An Indian yell came ut of the night and a racket of flight and broken ranches narrowed his stare as a man burst from brush venty yards to the right and came plunging headlong ward the blurred shapes of Travers' held horses.

Either he didn't see Travers or was too panicked to are.

Travers moved out from behind the roan with a fisted un. "You can stop right there!"

But the harried man didn't stop. Flame ripped from is middle in repeated orange stabs. Travers let go of e pitching mounts. The fellow was ten feet away, ill levering his Winchester, when Travers squeezed off nd saw him spin to drop loosely, roll once and lie ill with an arm doubled under him.

Travers toed him over and was bent with cupped match hen the Indian came up and peered into the dead ce of Wimpy Sellers.

Travers dropped the spent match. "Hate never ended an unsettled account." He got to his feet. "No-ning more we can do for him. Guess I've lost you a orse."

"Me find," the Yaqui said, and trotting into the gloom fted his voice in the yelp of a coyote. Three times e called and a yelp came in answer.

He was back with his mount when the others re-ined them. "Two fer one ain't so bad," commented hinnan, looking down at Travers' targeted ridge runner. That shortest Injun won't be wantin' no breakfast."

Travers saw the big Yaqui give the man a hard loo[k]
He turned to count noses. Shinnan caught his expressio[n]
"Hell, you can't boil a puddin' without breakin' egg[s]
What you figger t' do with this carrion?"

"Leave him for the rest of Crescent's enemies [to]
think about. But we're burying the Indian—come on. Le[t's]
get at it."

It was crowding twelve when at last they came in [a]
roundabout fashion to the cache of food Sellers' gunni[es]
had taken from the departed homesteaders.

Could that really have been only three nights ag[o]
It was hard, Travers reflected, to think so much cou[ld]
have happened in so short a while, to know the shap[e]
of tomorrow had been so drastically altered. By th[e]
conscience of a woman he'd likely never see again.

The argent disc of a three-quarters moon was lif[t]
ing above the boulder strewn hills which framed Apach[e]
Pass and concealed Fort Bowie when, in chilly gloo[m]
the group staved off sleep to get what good they cou[ld]
from cold jerked beef washed down with tinned tomatoe[s]

Travers wouldn't risk a fire, even forbade the solac[e]
of hand rolled smokes. "If McCartrey's bunch are on th[e]
move," he said, "we'd be goddam foolish to let the[m]
think they haven't yet got this range in their pocket[.]
No more talk. They've got to come this way to get [to]
the lake and I don't want nothing to upset their we[l]
come."

They had skirted the burnt-out headquarters gettin[g]
back to this place without turning up either Lupita [or]
Reider, and he worried about this as he chewed th[e]
tough meat. She might, of course, have decided to sta[y]
over. After what she'd been through he couldn't honestl[y]
blame her but he would like to have had the kid's gu[n]
to bolster the clash he knew could come any momen[t]

Whatever the cost, they had to turn back those cow[s]
each man waiting with an unrolled slicker.

116

"All right," he said gruffly when they finally were done. "Three shots will be the signal. Don't move ahead of them. Don't plug anybody if you're able to avoid it. What law there is we want on our side. Take off."

The men eased away one by one with their horses. Each had his position fanned across this ridge, placed to give maximum advantage to a yelling charge with slickers. Nothing elaborate about it; the plan was pared to absolute essentials. Simply panic the herd, then keep it moving. Those who were able, once the business was over, would rendezvous here to wait for the sheep.

Left alone in the night with his uncomforting thoughts Travers took on a bad case of the jitters. He had made up his mind about Lupita at last and her unexplained absence weighed heavily on him. Had they run into trouble on the road or at Willcox? Had they run afoul of the law for some reason? Were they captives somewhere, hostages to Ballard? A dozen possible answers disturbed his anxious thoughts. The worst was not knowing, forced to make this fight blind.

But one thing he knew. He was all through with running.

Waiting out the dragging moments, eyes scouring the moonlit distance, he felt again the startling impact of Pita's mixed-up personality. Fire and ice. Tempestuous, attractive, shapely and unsettling, she was all the things a man could dream of hunkered by some lonely blaze. She was indubitably the nearest thing he could expect to find for himself in a life's companion, the tawny glow of her Indian blood tempered if not refined by the stolidness of her father's Dutch forebears.

Glance suddenly arrested by the blur of distant motion, he pinned his stare more fiercely on the silvered wash of a serrated bluff. Ten minutes of watching confirmed his appraisal. The compact huddle of the drifting mass was unquestionably cattle, Star Cross on the move to take over Crescent's lake, five miles back of his dug-in vedettes.

Travers picked out the dark dots of the Star Cross crew flanking the herd as the mass drew nearer, three at spaced intervals well out ahead as skirmishers.

These posed a problem he had not foreseen, but there was no help for it. He'd have to let them come on, get within easy pistol range before making his move if his plan was to stand any chance of success. Those cows had to be panicked. Surprise, to effect this, had to be complete.

Three shots was the signal. Perhaps, with luck, he could put them afoot, though it chewed at his soft spot to kill offenseless horses.

He had Shinnan next left of him east down the ridge but a quick look that way failed to pick the man up. If the snaggle-toothed bastard slipped a joker in this deal he had better take off before Travers caught up with him.

The cold malevolence he had sensed in the man came again to take hold of and gnaw at his nerves.

Cursing under his breath he peered once more toward the herd, rumble of hooves a rugged throbbing in his ears. He could make out the eyes of the lead steer now and, bellied flat against the ground, brought up his rifle. With Shinnan on his mind he dared not wait longer.

XXIII

THE STAR CROSS scouts—three out in front—came poking along as though no danger existed, drawn together in gossip to hash over old stories, near enough to show the flash of their teeth when Travers squeezed off the first shot and, levering swiftly, fired twice more.

The middle horse went down, throwing its rider. The man to the right, yelling curses, got trapped in his saddle, pinned by a leg under the belly of his mount. The third man, whirling, got his horse straightened out and took off shouting, bent flat and spurring for all he was worth.

Someone else dropped the horse in a cartwheeling sprawl, then Crescent was up, slickers flapping and running, yip-yipping, straight into the face of the frozen herd.

Tails up, the whole mass spun about in its tracks and, bellowing with terror, wheeled away like a juggernaut in wild stampede as the Yaquis opened up with their .45-90s.

Travers called the men back. If he'd had his druthers he'd have chased that herd into Ballard's dooryard but the horses were too pooped for anything like that.

"That third whippoorwill's too dead to skin," Shinnan called, coming up.

Travers, scowling, growled, "Spread out and look for the one I put afoot."

They put in twenty minutes of mumbling unrewarded effort before Travers, too bone weary to hunt further, called it off. They were almost back to where they'd left their horses, Travers groggily discovering he was one man short, when the sharp flat crack of a rifle pulled them up.

Belatedly remembering the pinned-down man, Travers peered in that direction, seeing precisely what he expected. The two Indians followed him over.

Beside the dark blotch of the Star Cross puncher's horse Shinnan with his Henry stood cool as any well chain, waiting. The pinned-down man was just as unmoving and plainly would not move again.

Travers said, dust dry, "I thought I made myself pretty clear about this, Shinnan. I said not to plug anyone without you had to."

The man showed his snags of teeth in a sneer. "You think I was goin' to let that little bastard gut me?" He threw a knife at Travers' feet. "I was tryin' to work him loose when he yanked that out of his pants!"

Travers, bending, ran a couple of fingers between the dead man's shirt and the inside of his waistband. He straightened up. "A man has to be pretty reckless, mister, to pack a naked blade that close to his groceries."

Shinnan's saurian stare surveyed him in silence, hard and unblinking as agate. It shoved the burden of decision squarely back on Travers and he wasn't ready yet to call for a showdown. Not while that cottonmouth had both hands wrapped around a rifle.

Feeling meaner than gar soup thickened with tadpoles, he turned his back on the man and told his two Indians. "Bring up the horses. We better take a pasear along the rim of this holding." His drifting glance brushed Shinnan briefly. "No one but a fool would want to get himself found in the same place twice."

While they had time for it, he led them back first of all to where he could look down on Crescent's burned out headquarters. But there was nobody there, nor any sign the girl had returned.

With his uneasiness increased, the need for rest flapping against him like a frayed-out rope's end, Travers pointed his roan in the direction of Star Cross.

In another two or three hours the sun would come creeping over the rimrocks. Soon as Ballard's crew could get those cattle combed out of the draws and a herd put together they'd be back. They might even be heard from sooner. McCartrey and Ballard had a lot of face to save if they didn't want to find all the weak-kneed in this country snarling round them.

They might well come calling with unscabbarded Winchesters, too riled to care about how it might look. After all, Travers was only one man. Once they'd taken him out this wouldn't get to the courts. The girl they could handle, or would think they could, anyhow. She might even have been taken care of already.

It was this possibility that worried him most.

He couldn't go into court. If he'd had nothing to hide he could have ridden to Tombstone and talked with the sheriff or a U.S. Marshal and Ballard, mighty soon, was bound to figure out as much.

The moon shone on Star Cross, too. Ballard had more men to throw away than Travers. When they began to get near the probable route of the stampeded herd Travers called a halt. "Don't believe we'd be smart to go any farther. We're riding the rim of our range right now."

"What's over there?" Shinnan asked, pointing.

"Star Cross country."

"You goin' to set back on your heels while that bunch of range roughers get themselves pulled together? Christ, let's git over there! You'll never have a better chance to see that spread go up in smoke!"

"We're not going to climb into the same boat they're in. On Crescent grass we'll put up a fight when there's no way around it."

"Set back an' there won't be. You can bet on that."

"Nevertheless," Travers said, "any fight we get into won't be of our making."

"You keep doin' things the hard way—"

"Nobody's standing on your shirttail, Shinnan. Any time my doings upset your stomach . . ."

"Nobody with his tail in a crack could make any sense outa givin' them bastards enough rope t' hang a man!" Leaning out from his saddle Shinnan spat, brows beetling—but said nothing at all about pulling out.

Through wide open eyes Travers hung there regarding him, trying to build enough pressure to shake the man loose. But once again Shinnan sidestepped the obvious course. Above his taciturn cheeks the twisty stare grew mocking. "You won't git much done settin' there," Shinnan grinned.

Travers, inwardly cursing, spun the roan in its tracks. Skirting dark thickets of pear and stripped mesquite he led the trio to higher ground back away from the ruined look of Star Cross range. He needed to spread them out to make the most of what he had but, churned-up like he was, could not bring himself to trust that weaseling sidewinder out of sight.

Nothing that he could see had changed since they'd first clapped eyes on each other at Willcox. He'd been suspicious then. But the son of a bitch had him over a barrel and probably, back of that go-to-hell stare, was having himself a real belly laugh knowing that Travers —caught in this bind without an adequate crew—simply could not afford the luxury of firing him. Then, abruptly, it occurred to Crescent's boss the means of finding out lay ready to hand, and it was Shinnan's own words that gave him the cue.

"Rope enough," Shinnan had said. *Rope enough to hang a man.* And why not? He could at least make out to be doing what he ought to do. Split them up. Stretch them out, cut loose, to act as pickets.

By God, it was worth a try!

This way, unbeknownst, he could watch from concealment and—if the fellow was up to any kind of treachery—catch him flat-footed.

The plan was not without risk. Shinnan couldn't help knowing how Travers felt about him—it was the basis of those mocking stares. Shinnan had to believe he was free to act, that pressure had forced Travers' hand. To accomplish this and make it look reasonable there had ought to be a Yaqui on either side of Shinnan or, better still, Travers and Shinnan at far ends of the line. Big danger in this was that the Indians, with keener senses, might discover Travers' furtive movements behind them and cut loose with those cannons they were using for rifles.

Realizing it could go either way Travers made up his mind to take that chance. There was no way to warn them without tipping his hand.

He stopped the roan. "We can't afford to let them buggers get past. So we'll have to split up. If we had better light we might stretch it out some but for now, anyway, we'll keep half mile intervals. First shot means come running. You got that?"

Shinnan spoke up to point out the obvious. "They'll be a lot more likely to try it farther down."

"You're probably right," Travers smiled, "so we'll drop you right here. I'll hold down the anchor spot with our Indian friends between us. And let's not have any false alarms."

With a nod for the Yaquis he left Shinnan there darkly shadowed by mesquites and led off through the wash of pear fractured moonlight, turning loose the first Indian on a slope thick with creosote. The man's compadre he'd been going to drop off in a thicket of squatty cedars he remembered, but when these showed up he was too impatient to saddle himself with another mile of riding. "You go on," he said. "I'll stop here a while."

Soon as the sound of the man's horse faded Travers put the roan into motion again, pointing him north away from Star Cross till he could skirt with less care the first Yaqui's position. He bitterly regretted this waste of time and cut west again perhaps sooner than he should have, angling more and more south to come out above Shinnan.

He knew the man already would have had more than ample chance to move into his treachery. This harsh fact was too obvious to miss. But the main thing here was to unmask the fellow; any further moves could wait until he found Shinnan gone.

Confident of finding his suspicions vindicated, fed up

with caution and cruelly pushed by the need to get back Travers cut more corners and someway missed the mesquites he sought. He had to take time then to refigure his moves and was brought to the conclusion Shinnan's station was farther west.

He cut back to higher ground. There'd be no false dawn with that moon up there and he was getting too close to the real thing for comfort when he got his bearings and spotted the mesquites. There was no sign of Shinnan.

His angry eyes searched the silvery view without picking up the faintest vestige of movement. This was what he'd expected but he had to make sure. Half measures had never been a long suit with Travers.

With mouth clamped tight he walked the roan closer. Thoughts black as hate, he moved into the mesquites, ducking to escape the thorny scrape of whipped-back branches.

He got the surprise of his life when a rifle belched flame, the charge whistling past so close he felt the breath of it. "Jesus H. Christ!" he swore, discovering now with bulging stare the shadow draped shape of the dark bulk confronting him.

While he fought to control the terrified roan the snaggle-toothed Shinnan came out of his crouch. His voice didn't shake. He said, thin with sarcasm, "Next time you try t' slip up on a man you better git off your horse." He stood rigidly still. "You can count yourself lucky. I don't usually miss."

When Travers got his mount mastered Shinnan said, "What'd you come back for?"

"Don't matter now—you've sounded the alarm. When those Yaquis come in we'll try something different."

Shinnan kept eyeing him, finally snorting. "Burnin' Star Cross out while they're huntin' them cattle—"

"They weren't all out there. If they heard that shot the sooner we get out of here," Travers said, disgusted "the likelier we'll be to live to fight another day."

He turned his head to listen, still watching Shinnan from the corners of his stare. The ghostlike quiet remained unbroken. Then abruptly, far away, they heard the pulse of running horses.

"I better catch up my nag," Shinnan said, and slipped away from him, dissolving into the black latticework of shadows with no more sound than you would get from a spider.

Travers drew a long breath. He scrubbed a hand across his face and felt sweat come away. Finding the fellow hadn't settled a thing. But it mighty near had. If the scream of that slug had come three inches lower . . .

With nerves still jumping he caught up his reins and led his horse from the thicket, finding Shinnan mounted. They exchanged guarded glances. The drumming of hooves was plenty noticeable now and two horsebackers presently took shape, breaking apart as they swept toward the trees. Travers hauled himself into the saddle and moved out to meet them, Shinnan following.

"I've thought up a better plan," Travers said. "I'm going up to the lake—you three find higher ground and stick together. Dig in someplace where you can spot their dust. When you're sure they're coming build a smoke for me to look at."

"What we do then?" the big Yaqui asked.

Travers looked at Shinnan. "This chap will have the answers. Don't let him out of your sight."

Daylight was on top of him before Travers sighted Crescent's burned-out headquarters. He could see more now, assess more exactly what Star Cross had accomplished, but found nothing changed from the last time he'd been here. The fire smell still lingered. There was no sign of life but he rode down anyway, gloomily wondering how to hold Star Cross off until Tee showed up with more guns and the sheep.

Though he circled the yard twice he discovered no fresh tracks. The girl should have got back from Willcox hours ago. His apprehensions gave him black thoughts to chew on as he forced the tired gelding up the boulder strewn slope to the stage road. Bringing the horse to a stop just short of the summit, standing in the stirrups, shading scrinched eyes, he stared a long while into the brightening east, searching the rims for any vestige of smoke.

But there was nothing. Not even a dust devil twirled its dun spiral above the spread-out waste of those empty miles.

He rubbed red-rimmed eyes, bleakly thinking of McCartrey, never doubting for an instant that Star Cross would hit back. Ballard had no alternative. He had to have Crescent's water to survive.

Twisting around in the saddle he sent his stare toward the lake, blinked and looked again with sudden breathless attention at those gesticulating shapes, light-headed with the surge of relief that rushed through him.

He put his horse down the slope.

They met him in the yard. He cried harshly, "What the hell kept you?"

Quick eyes searched his face. Red lips smiled. "We've been camping out—I fetched a tent back to sleep in. How do you like this get-up?" She twirled in a swirl of skirts, but it was the scowling kid· that got Travers' attention.

Reider pulled a paper from his pocket. "Ever see one of these?"

Travers didn't bother opening it out; he knew by the size and look of the thing it was another of those Ehrenberg dodgers. He said, face expressionless, "You figuring to collect?"

The kid shook his head. "Found out somethin' else. They got a bounty hunter siftin' round these parts. Goes by the name of Fek Shinnan."

XXIV

"Yeah." Travers loosed a short laugh. "Newest recruit to Crescent's payroll."

He observed their shocked stares, the twist of a grimace tightening his mouth corners. "No sweat," he said. "Knew soon's I saw him he had some kind of axe to grind. I'll take care of him."

Reider showed more concern than the girl. She, apparently, had unbounded faith; but the kid, cheek chewing, asked, "What happens to this spread if he takes care of you first?"

Travers peered at him slanchways. "You wondering or worrying? I've not forgotten the deal we made. You've got five hundred coming. Any time you want to, yelp for it."

Reider showed color but said cool enough, "A bird in the hand never bit no one yet."

Travers dug out some bills and with the girl looking on counted his share of them into the watchful kid's held-out paw. "That make you feel better?"

"I was hired for my gun. Fifteen a month don't come near takin' care of it."

Travers stared at him, thoughtful. "You've been upped to a hundred."

"So what happened to Sellers?"

"Seems he bit off somewhat more than he could chew."

Reider dug his way through it. If he found anything he could take to heart the discovery did not alter his appearance. "You wantin' I should keep a eye on Shinnan?"

"I've got two Yaquis watching him."

The kid's curled lip climbed off his teeth but Travers, widening his glance to include Lupita, ignored this surliness. He had looked for the girl to come back from Willcox with a trunkful of finery and all she had fetched was this dress and a tent—not much of a spree for ten thousand dollars. She was showing more sense than he'd figured was in her.

He flattened his lips. "We've took on a new partner . . ." and let the rest of it go in the look of astonishment stiffening the shape of her.

The angry lift of chin, the darkening look of her eyes, made it plain as plowed ground what she thought of this high-handedness. But instead of the protests and/or reproaches he'd expected she said with a calm that set him back on his heels: "If there's any new partner he's yours, not mine. What you do with your half of this—"

"That's all right," Travers jumped in to say. "Nobody's trying to take anything away from you. If you want 'em you can even have my half of the cows. Chief thing now is hanging onto this place and we hadn't a chance of doing that without help."

Her eyes continued to rummage and peck at him. "Seems to me you been doing pretty good in that department."

"Pure bull luck. Be reasonable, Pita. Ain't a outfit in this country could stand up to Star Cross—"

"Not solo, maybe. But there's enough small spreads . . ."

"I thought about them. Wouldn't work and you know it. You'd never get enough of them to pull in one direction. McCartrey'd go through that bunch like a dose of goddam salts!" He dragged a sleeve across his jowls, finding this rougher than he'd imagined it would be. "Anyhow," he growled, "when Tee gets here . . ."

And came that suddenly to the end of his wind.

Between taffy colored hair and those red lips her black hard-staring eyes looked big enough around to ac-

128

commodate a six-horse hitch. He thought, *By God, they'll bust plumb out of her cheeks.*

"*Who* did you say?"

He felt like something backed into a corner. Ridiculous, he told himself, to be run out into left field like this. If it wasn't enough that he was risking his life at every turn of the wheel—forced besides to cut his stake in half—there was still that agreement he had screwed out of Lucey. And the ten thousand dollars she'd been glad enough to inherit. He guessed he had a few rights in this outfit!

"Phineas Tee," he said, much too loud.

Reider threw down his hat.

Travers spun, white with fury. "That's enough out of you! Get up on that rim an' keep your mind peeled for smoke!"

You couldn't tell whether Reider was going to grab for iron or not. For a couple of heartbeats it looked powerful likely some unlucky bastard would be mighty quick dying in the acrid stink of exploded powder.

The kid's stare grew wild and wavered. With a sound that came out in a half strangled sob he pushed a hand out in front of him, turned like he was blind, and, lurching, half stumbling, began breasting the slope that led up to the road.

Travers, plainly shaken, turned back to the girl.

She cried with scorn, "Did you have to do it that way?"

He could feel the sweat laying damp along his spine and the nausea still grumbling round through his belly. All he could see was the color of his anger but he pulled himself together.

"It says on my ticket my job here is ramrod. I'll decide what is best for us and I'll give the orders."

She hauled in a fresh breath, stare brightly defiant, hard and unyielding as the cut of his own. "You think we can survive tying up with a *sheepman*?"

129

"I don't think there's any other way that's been left open."

She stepped nearer to take hold of him, shaking him in her anguish. "Don't you *care* what people think? Doesn't it matter to you at all that—"

"The only thing that concerns me now is finding some way to hang onto what's ours." Travers, towering over her face, said, "With sheep we've at least got some kind of a chance. Tee's been achin' to get out of those mountains. Those sheep will help to hold back Ballard's cattle. With Tee for a partner we get the use of his crew, the fightin'est Indians this side of hell."

"You fool!" she cried, shoving him away. "Sheep will turn this whole country against—"

On the rim Reider shouted, wildly waving his arms.

Travers swarmed up the climb. "Smoke!" the kid yelled, running back from the road.

XXV

THE GIRL RODE with them, cradling a rifle, still in her fashionable dress and still glowering. He had tried to leave her behind and she'd laughed at him, harsh with the fierceness of the true *soldadera*. The contempt in her eyes when he'd mentioned the danger had shut off all his protests. "You think I can't shoot? Ask that bastard McCartrey!"

Regarding her covertly with the hiked-up skirt so uncaringly showing so much tawny thigh he felt himself blush. She was wilder, by God, than Phineas Tee's tattered Yaquis!

He pulled his thoughts away from her, peering off south and west without finding what he looked for. The

130

moke still showed above the haze of jumbled peaks,
ut no dust meant no cattle. Star Cross was traveling
nhampered, vindictive, out to crush once and for all
he frustrating source of its displeasure.

If they'd fetched enough hands they stood a good
hance of doing it.

They'd have seen the smoke probably quicker than
Reider, and McCartrey wasn't one to leave a stone
nturned. Left to his own devices he would stomp a
nake wherever he found it, and this lack of visible
lust on the horizon was proof enough he'd been given
arte blanche.

He'd go straightaway after the boys making smoke,
ut whether he'd divert his whole outfit or tell off just
, few of them was anybody's guess and, though he'd
vasted no time heading south, it bothered Travers. He
ouldn't leave those boys—the two Yaquis, anyhow—to
e rubbed out by McCartrey's range roughers, but going
o their rescue could be damned expensive if Ballard's
gun boss had split his force. It could be expensive either
vay, but once McCartrey had grabbed possession of
Crescent it would take some doing to pry him loose.
Vhich was why Travers had ordered the smoke in the
irst place.

When they got into the roughs, a cut-up country slash-
d and crisscrossed with barrancas and canyons, it was
lifficult to know which route to try. He had told the
ndians to find high ground and the smoke indubitably
vas coming off one of the crests off yonder, but seeing
t and finding it were two different things—he could
nly hope this would give Star Cross trouble. You couldn't
ell in these bottoms which canyon went where.

He passed up three before he found a trail plain
nough to look like it might be bound someplace. At
east it seemed headed in the right direction.

Half an hour later the canyon branched and there
vas no more smoke coming off the mountain. Who had

131

put the fire out could make considerable difference, but the big question now was which branch to take. Faced with the decision, this deep in the roughs, he couldn't even be sure which peak the smoke had come from.

Travers had taken definite bearings but what sparse glimpses could be caught of the heights from here, being from new angles, failed to turn up anything he remembered.

He seemed, in this country, to have a flair for wrong turns. Each time a decision had been forced upon him he had picked the road most apt for disaster. He had let Ballard's niece push him into inspection of the bone of contention, let the spread's isolation and roundabout quiet sell him a partnership in Old Man Pete Lucey's lake-fed jackpot—swapping ten thousand to shove his fool face into the hole the balls were bound for.

Settled in the driver's seat he had loped off to Willcox and picked three prime vipers to clutch to his bosom, ignoring the evidence of his own pictured likeness pointed out by Sellers before he'd ripped it from the tree. Oh, he'd played the prize ninny, no doubt about that. He had ought, by God, to be bored for the simples!

But none of this thinking offered much solace now. Probably neither of these forks would take them where he wanted to go, but since he had no way of knowing which of those peaks his boys were holed up on any choice in the matter was purely academic.

He took the right-hand fork because the underfooting here seemed a bit more labored, a little more likely to climb out of this trough. Several gullies led off to the right but he ignored these. Too late to turn back they rounded a bend to find the trail once more dropping, even twisting away from the direction he wanted.

They had now spent better than an hour in this maze and even if his Yaquis had managed to dig in they

132

could never hold Star Cross off long enough for Travers to get out of this and try some other route.

Cursing, he sent the lathered gelding on. When he'd told them to hunt high ground Lupita's whereabouts was his number one problem. He'd figured keeping them together would, at least for the moment, take care of Fek Shinnan while he took his look around. But he had not reckoned on trapping his Yaquis, forgetting that the smoke he had ordered as precaution against Star Cross might prove just as interesting to Deke McCartrey. Now he stood a good chance of escaping Shinnan's machinations and loosing his crew at the same fell swoop.

He pushed the roan harder. Minutes later, rounding another bend, he found the canyon doubling back toward its original direction, climbing now, bare walls giving way to ranks of ash and sycamore. Some bird, unseen, cried scolding protest and this patchwork quilt of branch-dappled shadows opened onto bare slopes enlivened by the twisted shaggy shapes of occasional junipers. A few saguaros showed among the rocks. One peak materialized dead ahead.

Travers eyed this carefully. In some odd way it seemed vaguely familiar but he could not find the remembered contours and, as they came nearer its closest flank, he pulled the roan off hard to the left. Skirting its jumbled rock littered base he was presently gladdened by the sight of another coming into his view some three miles beyond. At the same time a distant popping —a kind of firecracker sound which he recognized for gunplay—came down off the breeze whipped out of the opening between the two peaks.

"That's it!" Reider yelled, and hustled his grunting horse into a run.

Travers kicked the roan after him, fisting his rifle, leaving the girl to look after herself. The racket of gunfire was now plainly evident. As he got nearer tiny blotches of smoke ballooned out of the rocks two-thirds of the way up to reveal how close McCartrey had come to putting this part of Crescent out of business.

Unable on his harder used horse to overtake Reider, Travers dropped back to let the girl come up with him. He had his eyes on the rim, studying anxiously, worried by the sparsity of shots from up there. Already the kid had gone out of his sight around the back end of this knob's rocky slope. "Only chance we've got," he told the girl grimly, "is to catch those yahoos between two fires. If you can locate and run off their broncs it'll help."

He didn't wait for any argument—time was too precious. Feeding steel to the roan he drove it toward the closest rocks. He was down before it pulled out of its stagger, steadying his Winchester, hunting for targets.

His first shot whined off rock, utterly wasted. He had the range then and his second propelled a yelling man to his feet and a shot from the rim cut the legs out from under him. Travers, catching the glint of a rifle, squeezed off another and a second McCartrey hireling erupted from his nest to pile up limp against a rock.

A splatter of chips off the stone he was draped against drove him into a more careful cover. The whine and slap of plummeting lead kept him pinned down until the rifle went dry.

An increase of firing and a jumble of yells coming faintly from the far side of the slope gave evidence that the kid had finally got into action. Something moved in a clump of rabbit brush just under the rim and Travers jumped another man into the open to catch red hell from one of the defenders. He squeezed off another and, doubled over, plunged across ten yards of shale to drop behind a clump of manzanilla.

Reloading, he wormed his way under the branches to tip up his rifle without finding an exposure. Evidently, Star Cross, made aware of the precariousness of their vulnerable position, were seeking to find new ways and answers. A concerted shout from the slope's back side jerked Travers' head and a smile crossed his teeth as a twist of dust driving south across shale revealed several spooked and hard-running riderless horses. Yells and curses broke out of the concealed men above him and, to add to their joy, he emptied his Winchester, spraying the slope with a cacophony of ricochets. One of these found flesh. A spread-armed man staggered up and collapsed to hang head down across a pockmarked boulder. Echoes faded into a prolonged silence.

Travers lay there and sweated for another ten minutes without catching faintest glimpse of anything to throw a shot at. Things appeared to have reached a Mexican standoff. Then he got to wondering if Star Cross, rattled perhaps by loss of their horses or thinking what a chance this gave them to take over Crescent, had pulled out.

He wriggled out of his cover and, to test this, got onto his knees and with nervous care raised up to look around. No shots rang out; no glimpse of movement caught his eye.

Had Star Cross pulled out?

Travers, badly puzzled, stepped fully into the open without drawing fire. Knuckling sweat from red eyes he turned around, peering harder, without discovering a thing he hadn't looked at before.

What the hell was McCartrey up to?

Even with the fight going suddenly against him it didn't make sense that he'd abandon this chance while ...

A shout from the rim snapped his head up to find the bounty hunter's face staring down at him. "They've got the girl!" Shinnan yelled.

XXVI

WITH WHAT PATIENCE he could muster Travers waited while Shinnan, left arm tied in a bloody sling, came cautiously down through the jumble of rocks. With the girl for hostage McCartrey had knocked all the props out from under him. Unless they could snatch her back, and quick, Crescent was finished, everything he'd put into this flushed down the drain.

"How the hell did they get their hands on her?" he glowered when Shinnan at last limped over to swap stares with him. "Afoot—"

"She fumbled it. Too much of a hurry—didn't half run 'em off. Too anxious to get in her licks, I reckon," Shinnan said, disgusted. "Last I saw she was off her horse, chargin' up that slope with her hands full of Winchester. Next thing I know two guys had hold of her and another, further out, was fetchin' up their horses."

"Is this all that's left of us?"

"We've still got a Injun—he's up there pilin' stones on the other one."

"What happened to the kid?"

Shinnan shrugged.

Travers, scowling, sent a narrowing glance in the direction of Crescent, keeping Shinnan well focused in the corners of his stare. "Looks like we've had it."

"They could git overconfident. Four-five nags out there in the catclaw if a feller could latch onto 'em."

But it wasn't the horses that was gnawing at Travers behind the hard facts of Lupita's abduction. It was difficult to see how Shinnan could have managed this

136

Travers, not hankering for any more surprises, allowed, "We better start trying. But first," he said, pushing out the words as softly quiet as spider's feet, "don't you reckon it's about time to make your play?"

The bounty hunter, grinning, didn't pretend to misunderstand. Didn't stiffen up, either, or appear at all discomfited. "Finally got me pegged, eh? Noticed you been workin' at it." He lounged the rifle against a leg to scrub a hand across his cheeks.

Travers watched him, waiting.

"Cool as a well chain, ain't you?" Shinnan, showing discolored teeth, shifted his chaw from one pouch to the other. "I'm a businessman, Travers. Figgered we might sort of hatch us up a deal. Kinda 'bargain special' as the counter jumpers say."

"You don't have to promote it."

Shinnan's stare winnowed down. "How's two thousan' sound? For cash in hand we could fergit I ever saw you."

Travers said skeptically, "How long?" and Shinnan's quick mind pushed out another grin.

"Sounds like you been in this bind before," he said, waggling the hand that had been clamped around his rifle. "Nothin' up my sleeve. I'll even lean your way in this tussle with Star Cross. Fek's word is as good as his bond—ask anyone."

Two pairs of eyes shared unreadable scrutiny.

Travers dug out his money belt, thought a bit longer and crammed it unopened inside his damp shirt. "An honest bastard's something new to my experience, but I'll say this much. If we're both still around when this business is done with I'll give some hard thought to it. Meanwhile," he added, holding Shinnan's stare, "if you decide on cold turkey make your first shot count because you won't get another."

They lost half an hour rounding up four horses.

"Probably taken her to Star Cross," Travers observed "but we can't waste time on snap judgment guesses. You're the tracker, Shinnan. Lead off and get at it."

The man didn't look to be in half the impatience that was gnawing at Travers but the boss man of Crescent kept right on pushing. It had crossed his mind that McCartrey was not above staking out an ambush but he did not let this thought slow them down any. The broiled air in the canyon must have crowded 120 degrees but Travers' biggest worry was getting trapped in a wrong turn. Pulling his lead horse he kept crowding the heels of the grumbling scalp hunter, leaving the Yaqui to bring up the drag.

Wherever a passage opened up on the left he gave this terrain his closest inspection and this vigilance paid off. Shinnan, it seemed, might have charged straight on but Travers' yell pulled him around to peer at fresh sign heading south up the fourth left-hand gulch they came onto.

"They've split up," Travers grunted, bending low in the saddle, putting together the story of these tracks. "Biggest amount of them turned off here."

"We'll try it," Shinnan nodded, scowling as once more he put his horse out in front.

"Snap it up!" Travers growled, yanking the lead rope and kicking his mount back into a run.

The low walls presently fell away and they came onto an open flat stretching ahead for perhaps a long mile where flanking hills, pinching in, funneled the trail through a tortuous pass that was blue with bent shadows.

Travers pushed ahead, impatient with the bounty hunter's dawdling. The tracks were plain going into this gut and, spurring, Travers plunged into it after them.

Sudden shock raced through the saddle beneath him. The sharp crack of a rifle smashed through the clatter. Travers' gelding lurched, recovered and, ears flat, reaching, tore on through the uproar. Pounding hard behind im, Shinnan, waving his smoking Henry, pulled nearer. That one," he yelled through a snaggle-toothed grin, won't be botherin' no cook for second cups in the mornin'!"

Travers, eyeing torn leather at the fork of his hull, pulled his chin up and round, discovering that Shinnan, both arms swinging free, was no longer fretted with the ruse of that sling. His left arm between wrist and elbow was wrapped in a shirttail displaying dried blood but did not appear to be noticeably impaired.

Chalk one up for Shinnan.

Travers gave him that freely, yet was not lulled by the man's alacrity into imagining his intentions had very much altered. He was sure in his bones when the sign looked right this snaggle-toothed gore hound would make his play—would have gone the same gait even had Travers been fool enough to swallow that hogwash he'd peddled. Only thing improved by two thousand pocketed would have been Shinnan's appetite.

The world was older and filled with change but the same dark lusts swept folks today that had rushed through Cain when he slew Abel.

It was suppertime when, with the others behind him, Travers drew up to have his look at Ballard's headquarters. The power and influence of this big outfit was scarcely evidenced by things in view. More buildings, bigger corrals perhaps than a man would find among his neighbors, but no more wasted on ostentation. The buildings had been built of unpainted wood, rough sawed and frugal to the point of meanness. Except for size—it was three rooms larger—Ballard's house wasn't any more inviting than the barracks-like shack thrown up for the hands.

By the porch three horses stood spraddle legged, heads down, still heaving. Somehow the remembered face of Ballard's niece became superimposed on his pictures of Pita tied up someplace inside. It tangled his thinking and steepened the perils of what he had ridden here to accomplish.

His lips tightened grimly as he considered the placement of things spread before him. There simply wasn't any way to insure a bloodless victory. Two hundred yards of open had to be crossed this side of cover and no amount of staring would reduce these odds by so much as an inch.

Travers let go of the lead rope. "Let's go!" he growled and kicked in the steel.

XXVII

THERE WAS NO WAY of knowing if this bunch had got set.

Travers' head was so crammed with bursting thoughts obscured by others before he had any chance to latch onto them he desperately knew the only hope here was to try and bull through on sheer grit and will power.

Besides the two who had fetched her there'd be a cook to contend with and probably Ballard who—from what could be gathered—left most of the range end of things to McCartrey. Pointed porchward Travers lifted his mount into a fierce lunging run.

Half the ground had been covered with them yelling like banshees when a carbine, poked through a bunkhouse window, swept the Yaqui as cleanly out of his saddle as though he had charged full tilt into a limb. Without thought Travers swerved, driving hard in that direction levering slugs at the flash of its windows, slamming the last pair into the maw of that wide-open door.

He flung off at the steps, plunged through, dropping instantly, triggering blindly in a crisscross of muzzle streaks ripped from the dark of this howling inferno.

Trail of fire tore across his left shoulder. The hat jumped on his head. A clanking jerk at his ankle set the rowel of his boot madly whirring. "Keep firing, you fool!" a voice lashed out in panic. "Don't—"

Travers, driving lead into the middle of that yell, heard air rush out of it, the slithery thump of a falling body. He was already moving, rolling back of the door. But there were no further shots.

A pulsing stillness closed down with a man's gagging groan coming harshly out of it as Travers, vision sharpening, made out the shape sagged against a far wall. The man pushed out a hand. "I've . . . had enough," this one grunted, and let go of his gun.

There was nothing then but the rasp of his breathing.

A gray stretch of limp apron said this man was the cook—there'd been just the pair of them. Travers, wondering about this, shoved to his feet, uneasily turning as the outside quiet pushed new questions through his head.

He peered round the door. Except for the one sprawled shape of the Yaqui there was nothing in the yard from this angle of vision but black elongated shadows thrown across it by buildings. A breeze tossed dark branches through a murmur of voice sounds, one of these lifting in anguished protest. A sudden acrid smell of burning cloth and wood hauled Travers narrow-eyed into the opening.

Flame was pouring from two sides of the house, Kate Ballard with Lupita standing huddled before it, and frantic half terrified horses trying to break free of the porch rail that held them trapped in the path of the wind funneled smoke.

Afraid they would tear the rail off and bolt, Travers,

swearing, lurched into a run. The last thing he wanted was to be stranded here, saddled with two females, when McCartrey and his outfit, drawn by this holocaust, came rampaging back.

Pita, hearing him, whirled, and Ballard's niece came round, green stare dark with shock. The look of her skewered him. *"Did you order this?"*

While Travers was trying to think of something to say that might beat a straight *no*, Shinnan—glance still held by something inside—backing onto the porch, set his rifle against the rail and bent to fumble at knotted reins.

Travers, registering darkening astonishment saw the man snatch off the horses' bridles, pitch them inside and, shouting, arms flailing, send them, hellity larrup, pounding out of the yard. "What the hell are you up to?" Travers cursed, starting toward him.

Shinnan's grin was wild, his stare brightly gloating. "Readyin' a welcome for that goddam McCartrey!"

Kate Ballard rushed at Travers, trying to tear the gun from his holster. Travers, warding her off, eyed the twisted face. "What's this all about?"

"It's that crazy Ballard!" Shinnan growled. "I had to shoot the old bastard. Damn fool wouldn't hev it no other way!"

He backed off a step at the look on Travers' face. "You think I was goin' to let the sonofabitch plug me? Jesus Christ, Travers! You act like a guy with a gutful of fiddle strings!"

"I told you plain we weren't firing this—"

"Yeah! Well, I don't walk into this kind of a fight with both hands tied back of me!"

Behind him a section of roof dropped from sight in a shower of sparks. Flame rushed from the hole in great leaping tongues, throwing garish light over everything, illuminating the yard from one end to the other.

The billowing heat drove him nearer to Travers, something inside darkly coloring his cheeks, turning the